UNRAVEL
Me

Kendall Ryan is the *New York Times* and *USA Today* bestselling author of contemporary romance novels, including *Hard to Love*, *Unravel Me*, *Resisting Her* and the *Filthy Beautiful Lies* series.

She's a sassy, yet polite Midwestern girl with a deep love of books, and a slight addiction to lipgloss. She lives in Minneapolis with her adorable husband and two baby sons, and enjoys cooking, hiking, being active, and reading. Find out more at www.kendallryanbooks.com

T0371400

Also by Kendall Ryan

UNRAVEL
Me

Kendall Ryan

HARPER

This novel is entirely a work of fiction.
The names, characters and incidents portrayed in it are
the work of the author's imagination. Any resemblance to
actual persons, living or dead, events or localities is
entirely coincidental.

Harper
An imprint of HarperCollins*Publishers*
1 London Bridge Street
London SE1 9FG

www.harpercollins.co.uk

A Paperback Original 2015
1

Copyright © Kendall Ryan 2014

Kendall Ryan asserts the moral right to
be identified as the author of this work

A catalogue record for this book
is available from the British Library

ISBN: 978-0-00-813400-6

Chapter One

I listened as my best friend, Liz, droned on about her latest fling gone wrong and his deplorable behavior. 'I'm done with men,' she declared through the phone.

I choked on my latte, nearly spitting the lukewarm liquid on my computer screen. 'Sure, Liz.' She'd yet to understand that taking a guy home from the bar at two in the morning wouldn't result in a real relationship. I wasn't about to waste my breath explaining this to her for the umpteenth time. She was a contradiction in every way. Despite being a graduate student, her social life rivaled one of those girls-gone-wild reality shows.

'I'll just do what you do. Battery operated boyfriends never let you down, right, Ashlyn?' She chuckled.

I roughly swallowed my mouthful of coffee. *Nice.* It was good to know what she really thought of me. 'I'll be sure to buy stock in Energizer then,' I teased her back. If you asked me, Liz's sexual needs were off the charts. The simple satisfactions of working my way through grad school one crappy lecture at a time and an occasional fling with my vibrator kept me content…for the most part.

A new email in my inbox caught my attention. It was from Professor Clancy, titled *Possible Thesis Topic?*

I pulled the phone from my ear, cutting off Liz's rant to read the professionally worded message, inwardly cringing that I'd just been discussing vibrators. The sad thing was, Liz was right. It was the only action I'd had in two years. I just didn't have time for a relationship and casual sex had never interested me. I needed a connection before I'd get naked and share my body with someone.

'Liz, I've got to go. Call you tonight.' I hung up without waiting for her response, but could hear her laughter through the line as I ended the call.

I closed my laptop and dialed Professor Clancy's office number since he could be counted on to be there practically at all hours. Professor Clancy was a legend on campus and in academic circles, and I was lucky to have him as my adviser. He picked up on the third ring.

'I got an interesting call from Dr. Andrews,' he said. His calls always began this way--no *hello, how are you*--just straight to the point. 'And based on a patient he's seeing, I might have a lead on a test subject for your amnesia thesis.'

We'd been brainstorming thesis ideas that would also secure me a grant and allow me to work on getting a paper published in behavioral psychology, which was my field of study. Ever since I was a girl, I'd been fascinated by amnesia. Sometimes I fantasized about what it would be like to have amnesia, to forget all the painful memories from growing up. I realized Professor Clancy was still speaking and I listened as he described the man who'd been brought in to Northwestern Memorial Hospital several days before without a single memory..

'You're a genius, Professor Clancy. That's perfect!' I knew this assignment was meant for me. I could already see it – my name and an amnesia study printed in a medical journal. If that didn't prove that I'd made something of myself, then nothing ever would.

'There's one hitch though.'

'What's that?'

'He's under arrest for a murder he has no recollection of committing.'

2

I picked at my nails and waited for him to continue.

'He was arrested at the scene of a murder, standing over a man who'd been beaten so badly he had to be identified through dental records.'

I shivered involuntarily. 'Geez.'

'Yeah… You might want to rethink this, Ash.'

'No. I want to work with him.'

'I figured you'd say that. I just wanted to warn you and make sure you understood what you'd be getting into.'

'Understood. Thanks, Professor. Have they discovered anything else about him?' I asked, anxious to learn all I could.

'He recalls nothing of his life before. Not even his name.'

'That sounds promising.' We'd been kicking around the idea of studying the effects of amnesia and its psychological impacts, but the access to subjects was limited. I wanted to write about something fresh and cutting edge, not just regurgitate the articles already published in tired old journals.

'I've arranged a visit with Dr. Andrews, who's his attending physician. You free in the morning?'

'Of course.' Even if I'd had plans, I would cancel them to meet the amnesia subject. My stomach tingled with excitement.

I reviewed the file Clancy had emailed over, and prepared myself for my first meeting with John Doe.

I balanced my mug of coffee on the edge of the pedestal sink, and finger-combed my hair. Getting the long, unruly strands to cooperate was a daily challenge. I usually opted for a ponytail, but today I needed to look professional, so I did my best to smooth it down and tucked it behind my ears.

I swiped tinted moisturizer over my cheeks and mentally ran through the information in the file Professor Clancy had sent. The subject was a Caucasian male in his early twenties, six foot one,

one hundred ninety-two pounds, and most noteworthy of all, had absolutely no memory. He was suffering from complete amnesia. His file claimed he had emotional issues, which I expected as a result of the trauma. He had above-average intelligence and was articulate, yet had been uncooperative and withdrawn. He bore no distinguishing birthmarks, was in good health, had two tattoos, and was circumcised. It felt like an invasion of privacy knowing so much about him, but the prospect of meeting him excited me.

I had been too nervous to eat, so the slice of toast I'd made earlier sat cold beside my laptop. I tossed it in the trash and grabbed the file I'd printed out before hustling out the door. I might as well benefit from my inability to sleep in and get to the hospital early.

I walked the twelve blocks to Northwestern Memorial on Huron Street. After I'd moved here from Michigan last year to study with Professor Clancy, I'd sold my car, unable to afford the insane parking rates in downtown Chicago. Besides, I could walk or hop on the 'L' to easily get where I needed to be.

I took the elevator to the third floor. My legs were too tired to navigate the stairs after my early six-mile run and the twenty-minute walk to the hospital. Plus, it gave me a moment to collect my thoughts before meeting with Dr. Andrews. I hiked the laptop bag's strap farther up on my shoulder and lifted my hair off the back of my neck, trying to cool down. The doors slid open with a ding and I followed the signs to check in at the registration desk. The receptionist directed me to a consult room to wait for Dr. Andrews.

I sat down and grabbed the file from my bag, arranging the pages neatly on the table in front of me. The doctor was probably busy and would most likely keep me waiting for a while. Whether doctors were truly that busy or playing head games to make them seem superior, they always seemed to keep you waiting.

I needed to adjust to the fact that the doctor title would be added to my name in a year or so. Of course, there's a big difference between an M.D. and a Ph.D. I had no desire to be a medical doctor. Blood and bodily fluids? Ugh, no thanks. I cringed at the thought. No, I just enjoyed academics and studying. I hadn't really intended to get my doctorate, but I enjoyed college so much that I continued on after getting my undergrad in sociology and my master's in psychology. Then because I wasn't ready to do anything different, I applied for a Ph.D. program and here I was.

I smoothed down the edges of the papers to review the file again—even though I had it nearly memorized—just as the door swung open. I leapt to my feet and offered my hand to Dr. Andrews. He was dressed in a white lab coat and, with graying hair at his temples, he fit the conventional image of a doctor.

'Miss Drake?' He returned my handshake, pumping my hand twice.

'Yes, please call me Ashlyn.'

After exchanging pleasantries and a few stories about Professor Clancy, who Dr. Andrews knew quite well from their undergrad days at Loyola, he removed his glasses and rubbed his temples.

'I understand you're studying the psychological effects of amnesia and would like access to one of our patients.'

'Yes, that's correct. My goal is to complete a thesis proposal by spring term and I'd like to gather all the information I can through interviews and...'

'Slow down. I doubt Bob--excuse me, Professor Clancy--explained it you. He could barely contain his excitement over the phone last night, but this is a very sick young man. My advice is to *not* make him the subject of your project. He's dangerous, unpredictable and best left to the professionals.'

The condescending nature of his comment was like a bucket of cold water thrown in my face. All my life I'd battled people who underestimated me. People like me, who grew up in Detroit with an alcoholic, blue-collar father, didn't go on to become doctors by the age of twenty-five. That perception was exactly what drove me so hard--to prove everyone wrong.

'With all due respect, Dr. Andrews, I'm a Ph.D. student, not a high schooler working on a book report. I've interviewed prisoners before.' He didn't need to know that it had been for a project in graduate school and had been done via email. 'I can handle myself.'

He looked down at the floor, now aware he'd offended me. When he glanced back up, his eyes were clear, his face softer. 'Listen, Bob speaks highly of you and your work, and I want to help you out, but I just wouldn't advise studying this subject.'

'I know he's been arrested for murder, and that doesn't scare me. I have a thick skin, Doctor. I want to see him.'

'Very well.' He nodded. 'I doubted you'd be persuaded to walk away, but I had to try. It's clear working under Bob has rubbed off on you.' He offered a forced smile.

Professor Clancy was one of the most dedicated professors I had. He lived, ate and breathed his work. I respected the hell out of him for that.

'Here are his records, updated since he's been in my care.' Dr. Andrews handed me a manila file folder, already thick with papers. 'He's calm right now, but we've had some trouble with him.'

'Trouble?' I glanced up from his file.

'He was transferred here three days ago from the county hospital. His first morning here he attacked a male orderly who was attempting to give him an injection.'

'What provoked the attack?'

'He was shouting, demanding information about why he's being kept here, who he is, what we know about him. He has absolutely no memory of the murder. When the police came in to question him and showed him the crime-scene photos, he broke down. After that he didn't talk to us for two days. Then he just lost it.' He shook his head like it was that hard to believe this man would have trouble coping with a new reality. 'The guy he attacked was twice his size. Needed eight stitches in his face.'

I swallowed a lump rising in my throat.

'He's got some pent up anger and aggression. Consider that a warning about being in the same room as him, but somehow I doubt you'll heed that advice.' He smiled at me but his concern was obvious.

'Take me to him.' My voice sounded calm, even though this situation was rattling me. I reminded myself that if anything happened at least I was in a hospital, but the thought didn't provide any comfort.

Dr. Andrews opened the door and I gathered up my papers. 'He's resting now, but since you're every bit as stubborn as Bob, I'll take you in to meet him. I have no idea if he'll cooperate with you, seeing as how he's not my biggest fan.'

When we reached room 304, it was guarded by a uniformed officer. I stopped and faced Dr. Andrews before entering. 'Pardon me, Doctor, but I'd like to go in alone.' I had no idea where that idea had sprouted from, but somehow I figured the patient might be more willing to cooperate with me if I weren't with Dr. Andrews, since the patient didn't care much for him.

Dr. Andrews studied me, his eyebrows pulled together. He was old enough to be my dad, and I could see his concern was genuine.

'I'll be fine.' I placed a hand on his forearm.

He nodded reluctantly and signaled the guard to open the door for me.

I stepped inside the cool, dimly lit hospital room. Directly across from me, the man lay sleeping on a narrow bed, nude except for the white sheet covering him from the waist down. He had an erection in his sleep; his tense cock rested against his stomach and tented the fabric covering him. Aside from that, he looked peaceful.

I stepped closer, wanting to get a better look. He was strikingly handsome with messy brown hair, a chiseled jaw, full mouth and well-defined torso. His body was cut with long, lean muscles--not bulky, yet completely toned. His eyelashes fluttered against his cheeks and he let out a low moan.

It felt like an invasion of privacy standing here viewing him. My stomach danced with nerves, like I was about to be caught doing something wrong. Lying in the hospital bed like that, he could have been posing for a cologne ad. *Scent de insanity.* I pressed my lips together to keep from smiling, but that thought helped provide some much-needed levity to the situation.

I watched him sleep--this living, breathing, attractive man, who was so incredibly male. This contact with him provided a completely different experience than when I read his case file at my dining room table. This man was someone's son. A friend. A lover. Were they looking for him? Except, I knew from Professor Clancy that there'd been no missing persons reports filed matching his description. Whoever he was before had disappeared into thin air.

I felt something pinch inside my chest. *No one had filed a missing persons report? Who was this man? And what had caused him to block out his memory so completely?*

I noticed one of the two tattoos documented in his file. The name Logan was scrawled in cursive writing along the inside of his bicep. My mind immediately jumped to figure out who Logan might be. Maybe Logan was his brother or a friend, but really, who tattooed a friend's name to their body? Perhaps he was gay, and Logan was his lover. I pushed away the hypothesis that had no basis in reality.

His physical injuries had pretty much healed. His concussion was the only thing still lingering, along with a faint scar under his chin that was just barely visible.

The door opened behind me and I turned to give Dr. Andrews another earful about wanting to be left alone. Instead, it was a nursing assistant dressed in blue hospital scrubs carrying a tray with a plastic pitcher of water. I rolled my eyes. The doctor had sent this poor guy in to check on me, I was sure. The assistant set the tray on the bedside table and turned to leave. The man in the bed lifted his head from the pillow to survey what was happening around him. Perhaps uninterested in what was happening--or because he was drugged, I wasn't sure which--his head fell back again and he shifted to his side, cradling his cuffed hands in front of him. He flexed his wrists against the metal bonds.

The assistant looked from the patient back to me, and I offered a nod, signaling to him that I was fine and he was free to go, though my heart pounded steadily against my chest and I felt anything but calm.

I hadn't realized they had him handcuffed since his hands had been covered by the sheet when I first walked in.

'Wait.'

The assistant paused at the door and faced me.

'Remove his cuffs.'

For the first time the man in the bed opened his eyes and looked directly at me. I hadn't realized such a brilliant shade of hazel could exist until his eyes fixated on mine. I blushed at the obvious attention he directed only to me despite the aide hovering nearby.

Referring to him as John Doe didn't seem right. I'm not sure why, but with that name tattooed on his arm, I started thinking of him as Logan.

'Miss, I can't do that,' the assistant said, drawing my attention back to him.

'Do you have the keys?' I asked.

'Well, yes,' he admitted.

'Then yes, you can. Now unlock him.'

He shook his head, as if realizing he was in a room with not one crazy person, but two. 'He gave Terry a nice gash on his face, and you're too pretty, you don't want him unlocked.'

9

I turned to Logan. 'You're not going to hurt me, are you?'
He shook his head.
'See, he's fine. Now uncuff him.'
My dad was ex-military and had taught me how to throw a punch. I rarely got intimidated, even riding the train through the sketchier areas of town, and I wasn't about to back down now. I could take care of myself, and besides, I didn't believe he would harm me. There was something about him, some nudging feeling that told me I was safe with him. Even as I decided all this, I knew it wasn't logical. Clocking in at barely over five feet, he would tower over me by almost a foot, and if his muscular arms were any indication, he could take care of himself and anyone else in his general vicinity.

The assistant glanced at the door, seeming to wonder if he should go and check with Dr. Andrews regarding my request, or just do what I asked and get out of this room as quickly as possible.

I considered speaking up again, but he pulled a set of keys from his pocket and quickly unlocked the handcuffs before shuffling from the room.

Logan sat up in bed and rubbed at his wrists. 'Thanks,' he croaked, his voice deep and rough from sleep.

'You're welcome.'

I stepped closer and he drew the sheet up higher on his waist, concealing the trace of soft hair trailing down his belly. I felt mesmerized watching him.

My response to him was startling. Was I that starved for male attention that I was attracted to a good-looking prisoner? Damn, maybe my friend Liz was right--I needed to go out more, to get laid, instead of relying solely on my vibrator to do the job.

This certainly wasn't the most professional of me. I needed to speak up, explain who I was, why I was there, just as I'd done countless times before during the other studies I'd been part of.

Of course, those had always been led by Professor Clancy, and I'd just followed his lead, easily explaining that I was Ashlyn Drake, a Ph.D. student studying behavioral psychology and I wanted to ask a few questions. But my mouth refused to form the words, and instead I just stood there staring at him.

He seemed to have a question on the tip of his tongue, but he stayed silent as well, looking me over for a few long moments. 'Do…do you know me?' he finally asked. His voice was soft, inquisitive and I immediately relaxed at the sound of it.

The meaning of his question took a minute to resonate. He thought I was here for a visit. There was something innocent and sad in his eyes. Like they were filled with hope and wonder as he looked me over. Did he think I was his girlfriend? A friend? 'No,' I answered.

His face fell, and he went back to rubbing his wrists.

I stepped toward him and went to the bedside table where the assistant had left the pitcher of ice water. I picked up the plastic cup and poured him a glass.

I held it out for him to take, but he didn't react right away. He sat quietly, still meeting my eyes for another lingering moment before he reached out for the cup. His fingers brushed against mine. The warmth and solid feel of him startled me.

He took a sip without taking his eyes from mine. 'Why are you here and why are you treating me humanely? They say I'm dangerous, that I murdered a man.'

I sucked in a breath of air, forcing my composure to return. 'I'm a doctorate student, researching the effects of amnesia.'

'You're here to study me,' he said simply. It wasn't a question and his eyes flicked to mine, challenging me to disagree.

I saw my actions through his eyes, what he must assume were my motives for freeing him, giving him water, and suddenly my actions didn't feel quite so genuine. I'd need his cooperation, it was true, but I hadn't been thinking of my research when I ordered the aide to release his wrists, or poured him a cup of water. I'd been thinking of him as a man who needed comforting, which probably wasn't wise. It'd be in my best interest, and safer, to think of him only as a test subject. But it was becoming increasingly difficult to view him the way I should while watching him sit on the bed, with his chest bare and a five-o'clock shadow dusting his jaw.

I could easily rattle off facts like *approximately eighty percent of amnesia patients recover their memory*, but I couldn't comfort him, and that left me unsettled. I'd always dealt with statistics, scientific research, facts and figures, so being face-to-face with a guy my age, who I was undeniably attracted to, had completely thrown me off my game. I needed to pull it together.

'May I sit?' I motioned to the plastic chair across the room.

He shrugged his indifference.

Taking it as an open invitation, I pulled the chair closer to this bed and sat, then removed the files from my bag. Just this small act, having the papers in my hands, calmed me. I felt more in control, back to my professional self, and pulled a deep breath into my lungs.

I could feel him watching me. When I looked up, I noted the curious expression on his face.

'What?' I asked.

He shook his head, biting his lip.

I looked myself over, making sure none of the buttons on my shirt had popped open or something else awkward. 'What's wrong?' I felt too comfortable, more like I was talking to friend than interviewing a mental patient.

'You look too young to be a doctor,' he admitted finally.

Oh. I tucked my hair behind my ears self-consciously and glanced down at my lap. 'I'm not a doctor yet. I'm still in school.' And I knew I looked younger than my twenty-four years.

I read over the questions I'd prepared and suddenly, sitting in this hospital room with him, they sounded stupid. Too clinical. Besides, he wasn't likely to be able to provide the answers just now, so I'd probably only anger him. Not that I was worried about him becoming irate; I already trusted him on some strange level. I just didn't want to prod him with useless questions that would do nothing but frustrate him. I wanted him to trust me. And if I was admitting it to myself, I wanted him to like me. I closed the folder.

'I know you don't remember your name, but I'd like to know what you'd prefer I call you. John Doe just doesn't seem right.'

He swallowed and looked directly at me again. His eyes were piercing. I'd always thought the phrase 'the eyes are the windows to the soul' was stupid, but with him, that phrase held meaning. His eyes were rich hazel, with flecks of chocolate brown and deep, mossy green, fringed with black lashes. They were so expressive I could read his anguish at having no idea how to answer the most basic of questions.

He rubbed absently at the tattoo on his arm.

'Should I call you Logan?' I nodded toward the tattoo.

He ran his finger over the script, as if trying to decipher its meaning. 'Why would I tattoo my own name on me?'

'I don't know, I suppose you wouldn't.'

He nodded in agreement.

'I just figured it might be more familiar to you than John, though.'

'I suppose you're right. Even though there's nothing familiar about the name Logan to me, I guess I'd still rather you call me that.'

'Okay. Logan.' I smiled. 'Are you hungry, have you had breakfast?'

His expression betrayed his suspicion over my concern and I immediately felt guilty. 'Let's just get your questions over with, each day has been a parade of doctors, lawyers and investigators coming through here and not a single one of you can tell me

13

what the fuck is wrong with me. The sooner I can get out of here and back out in the real world, the more likely I am to remember something, right?'

Okay then. That's a no to breakfast. 'It's possible that certain environmental stimuli could provoke a response…' But I didn't explain that being under arrest for murder meant he wouldn't be leaving this hospital anytime soon.

'Would I know it if I was gay?' he asked out of the blue.

'I'm not sure. Studies have shown that sexual preferences don't change as a result of memory loss. Why? Do you think you're gay?'

'No. It's just… Logan is a guy's name, right? Why would I tattoo the name of guy on my body?'

It was something I was wondering about, too. 'You think maybe Logan was a lover?'

He shrugged. 'I don't know what to think about anything.' He lay back against his pillow and closed his eyes. I could see him struggling to keep his emotions in check. I couldn't begin to imagine what he was feeling, waking up one day in a hospital, being told you're under arrest for murder with no recollection of your life up until that point.

I noticed the dark circles under his eyes, the skin a pale lavender color. I wished there was something I could say, something I could do that would truly help him, but for all my schooling, lectures and textbooks, I was at a loss. I could hold my own in a discussion on the clinical symptoms of amnesia, but I had no idea how to comfort someone who was experiencing it. I wasn't a psychologist, I hadn't studied counseling, but suddenly I found myself wishing I had the right words to soothe him, to provide some hope, some semblance of normal. However, asking any of the questions I'd typed up this morning would just insult him.

'Listen, I'll let you get some rest. Would it be all right with you if I came back tomorrow?'

He nodded, and turned his head away from me, closing his eyes.

The conversation between us had been easy; he didn't seem uncooperative to me. In fact, his response to this situation seemed very normal.

I stood to leave, folding the papers into my bag. 'Bye, Logan. Sleep well.'

Just as I pulled the door open, I heard him. 'What's your name?'

'Ashlyn,' I answered.

'Logan and Ashlyn,' he murmured before letting his eyes drift closed.

There was something about his quiet nature, and intense gazes that stayed with me the entire walk home. The way he softly spoke my name together with his, touched me at my core. Like they were something concrete he could catalog and count on.

Chapter Two

The next day I returned to the hospital toting a canvas bag full of things for my session with Logan. A CD player and an eclectic selection of music to see if anything roused a memory from him, along with a collection of classic literature, the books most often assigned in high school.

Logan's case was not the kind of amnesia that resulted from a neurological disorder or head injury. His was a case of dissociative amnesia, essentially a mental illness involving the breakdown of memory and identity, making it all the more fascinating. I knew that dissociative amnesia was brought on by a traumatic event and occurred when a person blocked out certain information. Treatment options were extremely limited. They typically focused on relieving symptoms and controlling problem behaviors brought on by the stress and trauma. Now, newer studies were exploring how to help the patient begin to process and cope with the painful memories.

Since no one had come forward to claim Logan, even after the news outlets had a field day covering his story, I knew that family therapy was out. I decided to focus on art and music therapy, hoping to avoid going the medication route for anxiety and depression that Dr. Andrews seemed to favor. I wanted to see how far I could get Logan on my own. I didn't think it would be helpful to numb his brain with antidepressants.

Dissociative amnesia was by far the most interesting to study because the memories still existed inside the mind, but they were so deeply buried they might never be recalled. Sometimes the memories resurfaced on their own or were triggered by stimuli in the person's surroundings.

The guard stationed outside of Logan's hospital room checked my ID and nodded his approval for me to enter. I opened the door only to find an empty room. I dropped the heavy bag on the floor to stop my shoulder's aching protest and was ready to parade out to the reception desk to find out where they'd taken him, when a door on the side of his room opened and Logan stepped out in just a towel.

His gaze flicked to mine and he smiled. I was too stunned even to return his smile, with my jaw hanging down by my knees and all. His body was a freaking masterpiece that could easily turn any girl into a drooling sex addict. And glistening with water droplets, with that tiny white towel slung low on his hips, I was no longer thinking of him as a test subject. I was picturing what it would be like to have Logan's rough hands on my body, to feel the heat of his skin, to breathe in his musky scent and feel the stubble of his jaw against my cheek.

'Ashlyn?'

I realized that I'd just been standing here visually molesting him for God knows how long and I was about to stammer out an apology, when he turned to the side and I caught sight of another tattoo.

There was something familiar about the phrase scrawled along his ribcage. Without thinking, I marched forward and grabbed onto his hips, turning him to get a better look.

It couldn't be.

He chuckled at me, low under his breath. 'See something you like?'

'This tattoo. Do you know what it means?'

He looked down at the curvy text and shook his head. 'Haven't had access to look it up just yet. Besides I'm not even sure what language that is.'

'It's Latin.'

'You know it?'

I unbuttoned my jeans and eased down the zipper.

'Whoa, Ashlyn.' He took my wrist, stopping me, but I could see the heat building behind his gaze, which did nothing to extinguish the jittery excitement I felt. He ignited something in me. I thrust my jeans down just enough so I could show him my tattoo. *Aut viam inveniam aut faciam tibi* written in Latin over my left hipbone. The font on mine was smaller, but our tattoos were the same, complete with the curvy script written gracefully in black ink.

He released my wrists, dropped to his knees, and delicately ran a fingertip along the lettering that matched his own. He dipped his fingertips just inside the waistband of my white cotton panties, moving them aside to read the phrase uninterrupted. My stomach jumped at his touch.

'What does it mean?' His voice was husky and thick.

I realized I'd been holding my breath and pulled in a lungful of air before answering. 'I will either find a way or make one.'

The phrase had been etched into my mind long before it was permanently inked on my body. It reminded me to challenge myself, to never settle, and to push through my shitty upbringing to become who I wanted to be. It was a saying that would speak to those who had struggled in life and wanted better, and were willing to fight for it. I wondered what would have possessed Logan to have this marked into his skin. By the look on his face, he was clearly wondering the same thing about me.

He rose to his feet, and after trailing his fingers one last time over the words, he zipped and buttoned my jeans. I stood there completely at his mercy and utterly fascinated by him. What were the chances that we'd have the exact same Latin phrase on our bodies? The similarity was unnerving, but also interesting.

There were lots of things about him that were beginning to intrigue me. The way his green eyes followed mine, his musky, male scent. It also probably didn't help my libido that both times I'd seen him, he'd been shirtless. There was no way not to notice how attractive he was. My two-year sexual dry spell might have also contributed, but my body's response to him could only be described as primal...needy.

He appeared just as intrigued by me. He hadn't yet moved, and was still gripping my hips. I looked down at his hands, which he quickly dropped away. I took a step back trying to ease the sexual tension that crackled in the air between us.

He cleared his throat, mumbling something about getting dressed and disappeared into the bathroom again.

When he closed the bathroom door, I realized our encounter had left me light-headed and dizzy. When he'd leaned in close, the warmth of his skin and the light scent of soap had invited me forward, and I couldn't help but notice the way his sculpted abs and trim hips had barely held the towel in place.

I gave my head a quick shake. Now was not the time for fantasizing. I was not some hormonal teenager, I was a doctorate student, but I'd never been quite so taken with a man before. The experience was unnerving. I'd practically whimpered when his fingertips touched me. And I sure as shit shouldn't have unbuttoned my pants. This was completely unlike me and totally unprofessional. I rushed from the room as a sudden wave of panic hit.

I needed to get a hold of myself. I slipped into the ladies' room before my nerves overtook me. I looked at my pale skin and wide set blue eyes in the mirror. A frail frightened girl stared back at me. I splashed cold water onto my cheeks, hoping to add some color back to my face.

I took a few deep breaths and the color in my cheeks slowly began to return.

I had a decision to make. I could move past my obvious lapse in judgment of allowing myself to become attracted to him, or I could back out of the assignment and let Clancy know that I wasn't cut out for this. Then what would I do? Move home to Detroit? Find a job in the city? Work in an office from nine to five every day in a boring job I didn't care about? No, I had worked too hard for that. I was passionate about this research. Quitting now would be silly. I wasn't *that* impulsive. It would be fine.

I straightened my shoulders and took a deep breath. I would just have to do my best to keep things professional in his presence. At home later was a different story —I couldn't be held responsible for the Logan-induced fantasies that were likely to haunt my dreams.

After giving myself a much needed pep talk, I went back to Logan's room and slipped into the plastic chair near his bed. When I finally looked up at him, I knew my mistake instantly. I hadn't *allowed* myself to become attracted to him. I had no say in the matter. It was simple chemistry. A primal attraction that couldn't be controlled or turned off simply because I willed it so.

I took a moment to clear my head and focused on our work for today. I needed to maintain utmost professionalism with him. I had to set the tone and parameters of our relationship. He was in a fragile emotional state, and the last thing I needed to be doing was fantasizing about having sex with him. But God, I knew it would be good. That *he* would be good. He was entirely fuckable, and brought out my inner vixen in a way no man had before. I remembered his fingers on my skin, and mentally chastised myself for not wearing sexier underwear. A trip to the lingerie store at the mall was long overdue. I pushed the last lingering thought of his fingertips brushing across my belly from my mind and put on the most professional face I could manage.

After the fascinating discovery of our matching tattoos, we spent the afternoon listening to the various genres of music I'd checked out from the library. We discovered that he preferred rock music and blues over classical or country. He'd cursed when I put on rap and crossed the room to turn it off, which was funny. He made me replay a particular blues song three or four times, saying he was sure there was something familiar about it, but ultimately he couldn't recall anything specific.

Despite the lack of progress on producing any memories, the afternoon hadn't felt like a failure. It had actually been sort of fun. Logan had lain across the bed, his eyes closed, deep in concentration as I played the music, skipping through songs, or turning it up based on his preferences.

He asked me to leave the books behind for him to read, that way I was guaranteed to return to see him, he said, at least to pick up the books. If only he knew I was already anticipating my next visit.

The smile on my face had not faded when I ran into Dr. Andrews in the hallway.

'Have you been here all afternoon?' He frowned, looking down at his watch.

It was amazing that several hours had passed without my noticing. 'Um, yeah. We got a lot done.'

'Did he recall anything about the murder?'

Well burst my bubble. My stomach dropped. 'No. I'm not working with him on remembering that.'

He scoffed at my direct admission.

'Dr. Andrews, you're the one who diagnosed him with post-traumatic or dissociative amnesia. You and I both know that he's distanced himself from important personal information about himself and his life. His memory can likely be restored over time, but the events leading up to the trauma will likely be the last to be remembered. Or never remembered at all.'

Dr. Andrews shuffled his feet, still frowning.

21

'Besides, that's what the police-assigned psychologist is for.'

'Listen, Ashlyn, I'm only trying to look out for you. He's dangerous. You haven't read the police file.'

My belly danced with nerves, both wanting and not wanting to know what the police records contained.

'They'd found him in an abandoned warehouse, covered in blood, a sledgehammer nearby and the dead body of another man lying beside him. He'd beaten the hell out of him. Gruesome stuff.'

My skin broke out in chill bumps. I just couldn't imagine Logan being dangerous.

'He's a young man who doesn't even know his name, and though I appreciate your concern, I know what I'm doing.' I turned and strode towards the elevator, faking a confidence I *so* did not feel. I stabbed the down button several times for good measure, and when I turned around, Dr. Andrews was gone.

That night I lay in bed, looking over the curving script scrawled on my hip in the dim moonlight seeping in through the blinds. I ran my fingertips lightly along my skin, just the way Logan had. A low throbbing ache built between my legs, needing so much more. I let my fingers dance just below the waistband of my panties and imagined it was Logan's palm that was laid flat on my stomach. I closed my eyes and let myself imagine what kind of lover he would be. Through our visits, I was able to read his emotions almost better than my own. He felt entirely alone and craved comfort and closeness. Feelings I couldn't even let myself explore with him.

My fingers dipped lower, finding myself already wet. I stroked the swollen bud softly, as I imagined Logan would and moaned as pleasure rocketed through me. I never touched myself like this, preferring instead the efficiency of my vibrator, which quickly got the job done. But tonight as I daydreamed of Logan, I wanted to draw it out, to make the sensations last. To have his face in my mind and his name on my lips when I came.

Chapter Three

'The amount of time you're spending at the hospital isn't healthy, Ash,' Liz said, stepping forward to get in line for coffee. 'It's not normal.'

I opened my mouth to respond, and she held up one hand, stopping me. 'And don't say it's for your thesis. I talked to Clancy and he said you have plenty of outside material, and that your thesis outline is nearly done.'

I closed my mouth, unable to use the defense I'd been about to employ. I had a draft of my thesis outline complete. Logan's situation was only a small part of it, a real-life reference point in all the other data. It hadn't felt right to make his case front and center, dramatizing his pain that way.

I followed Liz towards the counter, needing much more caffeine to even consider discussing my relationship with Logan with her.

Over the last few weeks, I'd managed my schedule so that I could swing by the hospital and see Logan every day, even if it was only for thirty minutes between classes. My attraction to him hadn't begun to fade. In fact, it only seemed to intensify each time I saw him. But knowing I'd never be able to act on it, my feelings stayed bottled up. He was safe in the hospital for now, which made me feel the tiniest bit better. If he were to get out, though…I had no idea what might happen between us. Our sexual chemistry was ready to combust.

I had avoided elaborating on my visits to Liz, harboring a sense to guard what was developing between Logan and me.

'Tell me what's going on, Ash. This isn't like you to get so obsessed about a test subject.'

I swallowed hard. I needed to come clean about Logan. He wasn't just some test subject. He hadn't been from the beginning, and now after spending several weeks with him, talking music and literature, tasting all kinds of foods, I knew we had grown close. Too close as far as doctor-patient relationships went, even if I wasn't a doctor yet.

I suppressed a grin at the thought of Logan, struggling to keep my game face on in front of Liz. She'd jump on me at the first sign that something was off.

Even though my visits hadn't helped Logan to remember anything, spending time together brought him a sort of peace, he'd said. I provided a brief escape from his pain, and a break from the investigators who still questioned him, but were running into roadblocks as they tried to build their case.

I stepped up to the counter to place my order. 'Small skim latte.'

Liz barked her order to the cashier and handed him her card. 'I know I've been encouraging you to get laid, but I didn't mean with him. I don't care how good looking he is. He's a mental patient for fuck's sake.'

The dreadlocked cashier raised his eyebrows, looking between Liz and me. *Great.* I dropped my loose change into the tip jar and marched to the end of the bar to wait for my drink, clenching my fists at my sides.

We sat down in the cushy chairs in the back of the café, sipping our drinks. Liz's knowing gaze never left mine. 'Tell me what's going on. Since you met him, you've become even more of a hermit than before.'

I ducked my head, sucking in a sip of my latte. *Damn, too hot.* I knew she was right, but I couldn't explain the pull that Logan had over me. Maybe it wasn't healthy spending so much time at the hospital. I almost laughed at the obviousness in that statement. But Logan wasn't crazy. I knew that for sure. I also knew with absolute certainty that I'd be the one to go insane if our sexual chemistry got any hotter.

'I've got it under control, Liz.'

Each day I entered his room he lifted me into his arms and held me tight before setting my feet on the floor. I couldn't help but think that he was craving the physical affection after the weeks alone.

Dr. Andrews had seen us hug once and I'd instantly felt ashamed and embarrassed for letting myself grow so attached to a patient. Of course, it hadn't stopped me from visiting Logan every day. I just tried harder to avoid Dr. Andrews.

Over coffee, Liz tried to convince me that I needed to take a break from my work with Logan, that I was becoming obsessed. When she dropped me off afterwards, and saw the embarrassing state of my apartment, I started to think maybe she was right. Stacks of textbooks and a small mountain of notes had spilled from my overstuffed bookcase just inside the entryway, providing an obstacle to even getting through the front door. I had thought nothing of stepping over the heap the last several days, but watching Liz clumsily navigate it embarrassed me. I led her farther into the apartment, where at least the sofa was free of clutter.

She tossed her purse onto the couch. 'Seriously gal, you need to reel it in.' She waved her arms, motioning to the state of my apartment.

Despite any evidence to the contrary, my life was neat and logical. My piles of books and papers were concrete, things I could grasp. My kitchen contained only the essentials--coffee always left out on the counter and cupboards filled with cups of instant noodles. I didn't have time for fluff, for boys and their nonsense, and certainly not for the one I was studying who had more baggage than a celebrity's luggage cart.

But maybe my life needed the excitement Logan could provide. Things had gotten damn predictable--classes, boring professors, a drawer full of vibrators and romance novels dog-eared at my favorite scenes.

Still, against all common sense, I couldn't seem to keep Logan off my mind. With the criminal case against him weakening with each passing day, and the likelihood that he would soon remember his former life, I knew he'd be moving on and I needed to let it go. Heck, it'd occurred to me more than once with how good looking and charming he was that he probably had a girlfriend waiting for him, wondering what had happened. Although in my opinion, any girlfriend who didn't scour the city, search the hospitals, and jails and even under the overpasses for her boyfriend didn't deserve a guy like Logan. Period.

Still, it probably wasn't healthy to ignore my friends, and my poor apartment hadn't seen a vacuum in weeks. That realization smacked me in the face when Liz wrinkled her nose in disgust, weaving her way through the clutter.

'Okay, it's decided. We're going out tonight. Cocktails, mancandy, it's happening. Because, this--' She gestured to the wreck that was my home. '--is concerning. You need to move past Logan. I know you think you feel something for him, but it's only because of how passionate you are about your work.'

I'd told Logan I'd be back to see him after my coffee date with Liz. I hadn't missed a day since we'd met. Even though I didn't like the idea of standing him up, I knew there'd be no dissuading her. Besides, one night out wouldn't kill me. I could call the hospital and ask that they pass a message on to Logan that I wouldn't be able to make it today. That way, at least he wouldn't be waiting for me.

'Fine. I'll go.'

She smiled. 'Go shower. And I'll do my best to clean this mess up just in case you get lucky and bring a guy home tonight.'

'I won't be...'

She silenced me with a slap on the behind. 'Oh yes, you will. Now go.'

I took a brief shower and quickly shaved my legs, unsure of what Liz might be doing to my apartment. Despite being cluttered with textbooks and papers on every available flat surface, I knew where everything was. I didn't need her meddling with my system. When I emerged from the shower, pink and scrubbed clean, I found Liz sitting on the sofa, texting.

The apartment looked the same as it did before my shower. 'Gave up?'

She glanced up from her phone. 'Oh, yeah.' She waved a hand absently. 'There's no hope for this place. Just wear some damn sexy underwear, and hopefully the lucky guy won't notice or care that you live like an animal.'

I sent a quick email to the hospital receptionist on Logan's floor and dressed in jeans and a tank top. Liz helped me dry my hair pin straight and did my makeup, too, and then I hobbled on my seldom-worn heels to her apartment for some pre-drinks.

Around ten-thirty, we finally stepped inside a sleek lounge, an off-campus favorite that I hadn't been to yet. Liz kissed the bouncer on both cheeks and he swatted her backside, leading me to believe she was here more often than I'd thought.

We sipped on cosmopolitans in sleek martini glasses, and the combination of vodka and liqueur went straight to my head. Before long, Liz and I were gyrating on the dance floor to techno music, writhing together to the delight of a group of guys observing us from across the room.

When I could no longer stay steady on my heels without spilling my drink from the rim of the martini glass, I made my way to the side of the dance floor and slid into a booth. I slipped off the heels underneath the table and stretched my aching feet. I watched Liz continue to shake her booty and grind into the lap of an overeager frat boy.

I ordered a water and rested my chin in my hands, watching Liz enjoy herself. Sometimes I was jealous of her ability to embrace the moment and live life to the fullest. She didn't have a care in the world. Besides working, school, studying and reading, there wasn't much else to my life. Until Logan came along.

One of the frat guy's friends slid into the booth next to me, smiling at me with a drunken grin. 'Hey,' he called over the thumping music.

'Hey,' I returned. I was so not interested, but managed to engage him in conversation, mostly to please Liz who offered me encouraging looks from the dance floor now and then.

About ten after one, I was exhausted, tipsy and ready for bed. Alone.

I said goodbye to Liz, who was practically attached at the face to frat boy number one. She waved and made me promise to call her in the morning. As if she'd even remember this conversation, I vowed to call her first thing.

I stumbled to the street and began walking toward my apartment, confident that I could hail a cab on the way if I didn't feel like walking the eight blocks. And in these shoes that was a distinct possibility. At least I felt safe here. The streets were well lit with streetlamps every dozen feet and the sidewalks were fairly well populated with college students out looking for a good time. Not to mention a police officer or two could be spotted fairly easily if you were looking.

I passed by a Thai restaurant, glancing up at the sign above me with a gilded golden elephant. I wondered if Logan would like Thai food, or if tasting it would spark a memory for him. A smile pulled at my lips at the thought of bringing Logan here, watching him lick spicy peanut sauce from his lips. I felt lighter in his presence, incredibly alive and carefree, something that was rare for me since most of my days were spent worrying about my mounting student-loan debt, the endless research papers that needed writing, and even my dad who was all alone back in Michigan. At least tonight the alcohol left me with a fuzzy buzz and I could daydream about Logan on my walk home.

I passed by the small park I often sat in to read or study. It was little more than a cluster of trees and some park benches, but in the heart of downtown, you couldn't be too picky with green spaces.

The evening air was cool and felt great against my overheated skin and the nearly full moon made it a beautiful night. It would have been a nice night to walk home, if it weren't for these blasted shoes. I stopped to lean against a lamppost and removed my heels.

A policeman prodding a homeless man on a park bench caught my attention. The man sat up, and rubbed his hands across his face. It was the same mannerism Logan used when he was tired or frustrated. It had to be a guy thing. But then the streetlight caught on his bicep and a tattoo…. *Logan.*

It couldn't be. Yet I found myself jogging toward them all the same, heels dangling from my hand.

The police officer had roused the man onto his feet and was urging him along. Like a slap to the face, it hit me that this was indeed Logan. I didn't understand how or why he'd been released, but there he stood, in my neighborhood park in the middle of the night.

'Logan!' I called.

He turned suddenly, his gaze locking with mine. He looked tired, weary and untrusting. My heart sank. There wasn't even a question; I had let him down by not coming today. Had he snuck out to see me? Why did that thought make me deliriously happy? *Sick, Ashlyn, sick.* I was becoming obsessed with him and Liz was

29

right, it wasn't healthy. But seeing Logan here, the feelings he roused within me, I just didn't care. I needed to see him.

I jogged the last few paces and stopped in front of him. He didn't greet me with his customary hug, but instead stood coolly observing me. A pang of regret flared up inside my chest. I shouldn't have ditched him to hang out with Liz tonight. Especially when she was ditching me for guy right now.

The police officer cleared his throat. 'You know him?'

'Yes, I know him,' I said, without taking my eyes from Logan's. His gaze softened just the slightest bit.

'Just move it along, folks. No sleeping in the park.'

'No problem, officer.' I nodded, not breaking eye contact with Logan.

A moment later the cop turned and left, leaving us alone in the dark, silent park.

Seeing him outside the hospital was throwing me off more than I cared to admit, like he only existed within the walls of that tiny hospital room. 'What are you doing out here?'

Logan rubbed a hand across the back of his neck, looking down at the ground. 'They dropped the charges against me today. And then you didn't come…'

'I'm sorry,' I interrupted. I knew from overhearing hallway conversations in the hospital there was no case against him.

'And since they couldn't legally hold me in the hospital anymore, I signed myself out.'

'Oh.' *Oh* was all I could come up with. He'd chosen to be homeless rather than stay another night in the hospital. It didn't make any sense. 'Well, do you have anywhere to go?' I reached for his forearm and he stepped back, out of my reach.

'I'll be fine, Ashlyn. You got what you wanted for your paper. I heard Dr. Andrews say something about your thesis being nearly finished. I figured that was why you didn't come back today. You're free to go on with your life. Forget about me. Everyone else has,' he added under his breath.

I stepped in closer, placing my palm on his cheek. 'No, Logan. You've got it wrong. My paper's been done for several days. I couldn't come tonight, but I left a message for you with the hospital staff.'

He raised his eyebrows, like he was deciding if he should believe me. 'I never got a message.'

'I'm sorry, but I didn't ditch you. Come back to my apartment for the night. We can figure things out in the morning.'

He removed my hand from his cheek, lowering it to my side. 'I don't want your pity, Ashlyn.'

'Logan, we both know there's something between us. This isn't pity. Please come with me. You need somewhere to sleep tonight. Let me be there for you.' Those last words seemed to soften him, because he closed his eyes for a moment then nodded.

'Okay. If you're sure it's no trouble.'

I looked at the ground, my throat tight, and my stomach a bundle of nerves. 'I promise it's no trouble.'

I led Logan the few blocks to my building in silence, while the tension rolled off him in waves. I hated that he thought I'd abandoned him once I got what I needed for my paper. Couldn't he see that it was so much more than that for me? We walked up to the third floor, which I'd grown used to and no longer left me winded. I unlocked the door, and grimaced when I remembered the state of my apartment and Liz's warning about bringing a man home tonight. Who could have known she'd be right and that it'd be Logan? It seemed impossible, but he really was here, stepping inside my crowded one-bedroom apartment, his large frame making it look even smaller than it was.

I flicked on the foyer light, illuminating the crazy mess that was my apartment. 'Home sweet home,' I murmured, tossing my keys onto the side table.

'Wow. I can...see that.'

'And no cracks about my housekeeping. Despite the mess, I know where everything is.'

He chuckled. 'You don't have people over often, do you?'

I shook my head. 'Just my friend Liz. You're the first guy I've had here.'

'Really?' He seemed surprised, almost unbelieving.

'Yep.' I tossed my heels in the corner on top of my mound of shoes and motioned him toward the sofa. 'Have a seat. Can I get you anything? I'm going to grab myself a bottle of water.'

'Water would be nice, thanks.'

I grabbed the bottles of water from the fridge and when I returned to the living room, I found Logan standing in front of the single painting that hung on my living room wall, a print of Van Gogh's *Starry Night*. His finger lightly traced the blue swirls of the sky as if he was remembering some detail. He dropped his hand and went to the sofa at the end of the room. His looming presence dominated my tiny apartment, his handsome features contrasting with the shabbiness surrounding us.

We sat down on the sofa, sipping our bottles of water. My apartment was every bit the student-on-a-budget look, cheaply furnished with hand-me-downs and furniture from Ikea. But I felt comfortable here. I had two large bookcases in the living room overflowing with classic novels and my favorite textbooks, plus various medical journals. My couch was a rich wine color with throw pillows in bright shades of lime and tangerine. The coffee table was a pale wood with enough nicks and dings to make it inviting enough to put your feet up on. But at the moment, neither of us seemed overly comfortable. We both perched on the edge of the sofa, with several feet separating us.

Things felt strange with him here, outside the hospital room I'd seen him in every day. It was like his every movement was magnified, his forearms tense with muscles and veins as he held the water bottle. His scent was invading my space, and it was hard to pay attention to anything but him.

After a few minutes of uneasy silence, Logan stood. 'Ashlyn, I think I need to be going. Being here with you isn't a good idea. You don't even know me.'

I didn't point out that I probably knew him better than anyone. 'Logan, I want you to stay. It's late and we should both get some rest. You can sleep on the couch tonight, and we'll figure everything out in the morning. I'm not letting you go anywhere. You cooperated with me for my paper, and now I want to help. In the name of research, of course.'

He let out a deep sigh, knowing I was winning this round. 'So in the name of amnesia research, you're inviting me to stay?' His voice was tinged with just a bit of humor, like mine.

I nodded, solemnly. 'In the name of science, yes, I'd like you to stay.'

He cracked a slight grin. 'Then how can I say no?'

'You shouldn't want to.'

'I don't.'

Our conversation had too many twisted meanings and double negatives. Just his physical presence made my head spin and I couldn't be certain we were talking about the same thing. 'So you'll stay the night?'

'Yes.'

I claimed a small victory at winning this round. 'How could they just let you leave? Without anywhere to go...any money...? That's crazy.'

He ran his hands through his hair. 'Yeah, I suppose it is. But they couldn't legally hold me there anymore and I knew sitting in a hospital room wasn't going to help me remember anything. I'd rather be out in the city, experiencing life and seeing if anything sparks a memory. Or maybe someone might even recognize me. Assuming I did live here in Chicago.'

'I guess that makes sense, but I mean, what was your plan? Sleep on a park bench tonight...and then...' I threw my hands up in the air.

'Actually, no. Before I left the hospital they gave me the address of a shelter to stay at for the night and a social worker to visit in the morning about a work program they have for rehabilitating people. I just...couldn't follow through with it.'

I waited while he gathered his thoughts, not pushing him. Before I even realized it, my hand drifted to his and I lightly brushed the back of his hand.

He gazed up at me, surprised. 'Going through with that was like admitting I was nothing, a nameless, faceless nobody. With nothing to my name and nobody who even cares. It was too much.'

'I see.' I understood just what he was saying. Sleeping overnight in a homeless shelter would be a very humbling experience. I was grateful, not for the first time, that I had happened upon him tonight. 'You're not alone.' I squeezed his hand.

He looked down at our intertwined fingers, a frown forming on his face. 'There's something we need to talk about if I'm going to stay here with you.'

I nodded obediently. 'Come sit down.' I just wanted to keep him from fleeing. I couldn't stand the guilt of thinking he was spending the night outside on a park bench.

We each pulled out a chair and sat perched at the dining room table facing each other.

He looked me straight in the eye. 'I know my attraction to you has probably been obvious.'

A slow smile crept over my lips. *Interesting...*

'I know you could get into trouble if someone thought you were having an improper relationship with me. I need to let you know,

I'm not ready to pursue anything…with anyone. So if I'm staying here with you, we'll need to agree it's friendship only.'

'Absolutely, of course.'

He nodded his head, solemnly, and cleared his throat, taking his time. 'Thank you.' He nodded his agreement, but I knew this conversation was far from over.

I gathered up some extra blankets from the closet and the spare pillow from my bed and set them on the sofa for him. 'Hope these are okay.'

'Yes, thank you.'

I stood there awkwardly for a second, unsure what to do with myself while he looked down at me. 'I think I'll go change. Be right back.'

He nodded and watched me turn to leave. I grabbed my pajamas and headed into the bathroom. I stared into the mirror, having an impossible conversation with myself. What was I doing? Maybe it was insane to have him here in my apartment, but I couldn't see reason or logic where Logan was concerned. My instincts told me that he could be trusted. I stripped off my jeans, shirt and bra and changed into a pair of cotton shorts and a clean white tank top. I lifted my hair off my neck and secured it in a messy bun.

I'd thought about having Logan in my bed for weeks, and now that he was here, I was a jittery mess. I knew I'd never have the courage to make the first move, and he seemed unsure about even being here, so somehow I doubted my fantasy of getting him in my bed was going to come true, especially after his little speech about us being just friends. It both frustrated and relieved me. I wasn't one to make a first move, and my ego couldn't handle him shooting me down. Plus, I'm sure he had bigger things on his mind--like where he was going to live--and wasn't as sex-starved as me.

Chapter Four

I took a deep breath, pulled open the bathroom door, and headed into the living room. I expected to see him making a bed on the couch, but he was no longer there. I checked the kitchen and dining room. Both were empty.

His file lay open and scattered across the dining room table. Photos of the crime scene and an email from Professor Clancy were at the top of the pile. The email was brief, but contained a stark warning against getting involved with Logan, reiterating the violence at the crime scene. Damn it. I hadn't intended for Logan to see these. I rushed into the hall.

Logan was retreating down the hallway, but when I called out his name, he stopped and turned to face me.

'Please.' The one word plea was all I could verbalize. It meant so many things, please stay, please don't just leave me, please don't be the man they say you are…

He seemed to understand on an unspoken level and began walking toward me. I met him halfway, as if drawn forward by some greater force.

'Those things in my file.' He sighed and rubbed his hands across his face. 'I'm not safe. You don't even know me.'

'I know you better than anyone. I trust you.' I knew one thing for certain; I didn't want him to leave.

36

'Ashlyn…' My name on his lips was the softest sound. His gruff, deep voice was incredibly sexy.

'What?' I whispered, stepping in closer.

'About the murder…' He clenched his fists at his sides.

My stomach dropped. *Oh shit.* What if my instincts were wrong? Maybe this was a terrible idea. Logan didn't seem violent or dangerous to me, but how well did I really know him? He didn't even know himself.

'I honestly don't believe I'd have it in me to…do something like that. It had to be self-defense, but the truth is I don't know for sure. But I want you to know, you can trust me being here with you.'

The murderer said to the weak, young girl. I swallowed the lump in my throat, and met his eyes. They were sincere and kind, and locked on mine, seeking forgiveness. Trust. It was the one thing I had to offer him, after he had opened himself up to assist in my research. 'I know.'

He was quiet for a moment while he studied me. 'Thank you.'

'You're welcome,' I mumbled, looking down at my feet.

'I know I didn't deserve it, but it was your visits that got me through the past few weeks.'

'Me too,' I admitted.

He seemed shocked by my admission. He lifted my chin with his fingers. 'What do you want?'

'Stay here with me.'

'I shouldn't be alone with you. Maybe what they say about me is true.'

'I don't believe you're dangerous. I trust you.'

'Maybe you shouldn't.'

It was like a bucket of ice water thrown on my libido.

'I was your test subject, someone to study and experiment with to see how I responded. Was that all I was to you?'

'No, Logan. I never saw you like that. I probably should have. I'm sorry you saw that email from Clancy, but that was his warning because he and Dr. Andrews knew I was getting attached to you, and my friend Liz took me out tonight to meet a man because she said…' I stopped myself from saying anything embarrassing. 'She said what?' He quirked an eyebrow.

Shit. My cheeks flared crimson. So much for not incriminating myself with something embarrassing. 'She said I needed to, um, get some.'

He brushed my hair back from my face. 'You're beautiful. You could have any man you wanted on his knees begging for you.'

'Yeah right,' I mused.

He looked amused. 'So…did you? Get some, I mean?'

I looked him straight in the eyes, my lower lip pouting out just slightly. 'No.' *Okay, that was so the alcohol talking.* I was never usually this bold. But he had already admitted he was attracted to me.

He leaned down, bringing his lips flush with mine. 'We shouldn't do this,' he whispered against my mouth.

'I know,' I whispered back. My head knew I was crossing a professional line that wasn't appropriate, but damn if my body had gotten the memo. I wanted his hands on every inch of me. I leaned in closer, eager to feel him pressed against me.

His eyes stayed locked on mine, as he brought his hand up to cradle my jaw. His thumb skidded against my cheek, brushing my bottom lip.

My lips parted just slightly, in an open invitation to him.

'We shouldn't,' he breathed, but his eyes were full of heated passion.

'Please.' My eyes drifted closed as he leaned forward and pressed a single kiss to my lips. It was soft and careful, almost innocent, like a kiss between friends. Except his mouth continued to hover over mine.

I trailed my tongue along his top lip until he opened his mouth. When his tongue touched mine, a warm rush of heat shot straight between my legs and I let out a ragged moan.

Logan stopped suddenly and pulled back. 'You taste like liquor. Are you drunk?' He tilted my chin up, forcing me to meet his eyes.

'Not drunk, just a little tipsy.' I leaned into him, wanting to feel his mouth against mine again, but he hesitated to kiss me back.

'I want this, Ashlyn, believe me. I've thought of this since I first saw you, but not like this. Not when you're drunk. Not when you're unable to think clearly about what you want. You'll regret it.'

'I won't…'

'Hush.' He silenced me with a finger placed over my lips. 'Don't tempt me. My willpower can't stand much more.'

'So give in.' I smiled at him coyly.

He pulled in a deep breath and released a sigh. 'Woman, you are trouble.'

I slid my hands up his chest, loving the feel of his firm muscled chest under his T-shirt. My hands found their way into the hair at the back of his neck and I used the leverage to bring his mouth to mine once again. The kiss started out soft and teasing, just damp lips exploring each other, but soon turned wild and heated, our tongues flirting and tasting as we got more comfortable. He might not remember anything of his past, but I knew one thing for certain--he was a damn good kisser.

He pulled back just slightly, breathing hard against my mouth. 'Tell me to stop.'

I couldn't. My voice wouldn't come. I just continued kissing him, wishing this never had to end.

'Ashlyn, make me stop.'

'No,' I breathed into his neck, holding on for dear life. He growled near my ear as I moved my hands to his butt, pulling him firmly against me. I felt his thick erection press against my belly. 'Don't stop,' I moaned.

He pulled back from me suddenly. My lips were swollen and damp from his assault of kisses.

'I trust you.'

'If you knew what I thought about....you wouldn't trust me.'

My heart strummed in my chest. 'What do you think about?'

'All the things I want to do to you, but can't.' He ran his thumb across my bottom lip.

I sucked my lip into my mouth and held my breath. 'Like what?' I whispered.

He leaned in toward me. I thought he might kiss me, but he turned his head, leaning down near my ear. 'Being inside you,' he whispered against my hair. 'Making you come.'

My sex clenched at the sultry sound of his voice and a breathy moan slipped from my lips. Oh God, he was hot.

'But I won't do that. We can't.' He swallowed roughly, his throat constricting with the effort.

I rubbed my breasts against him, hoping to change his mind. My sensitive nipples rasped against his firm chest, which only succeeded in making me hotter.

'Please…Logan…' I breathed, continuing to rub myself against him like a cat against a scratching post.

'Not here.' He took my hand and pulled me into my apartment, kicking the door shut behind us and pressing my back against the wall. He kissed me senseless while I writhed against him. He gripped my ass and pressed his erection against me. I'm not sure how long it went on, but my panties were soaking wet, and I'd never been so turned on in my entire life.

I reached between us for the button on his jeans, but his hand found mine and stopped me. 'Ashlyn, no.' He let out a frustrated growl and worked to get his breathing under control. Then he pressed a kiss to my nose. 'You've been drinking. Please. Let me put you to bed.'

'God, yes,' I moaned.

He chuckled. 'I meant that I'd tuck you in to *sleep*.'

Oh hell. I'd tried and failed to seduce the one man I truly wanted. My chest suddenly felt tight, and I swallowed hard, forcing my emotions to take a back seat. I nodded my consent and untangled myself from him. I wouldn't cry, but damn if I didn't feel rejected, betrayed.

I headed into my bedroom, not bothering to turn on the light since the moonlight filtering in provided plenty of light to see by. I collapsed onto my bed, hoping he'd just leave me alone before I broke down with the tears that were certain to come. So, of course, he didn't. Logan followed me in, knelt beside my bed and helped me get under the covers.

I closed my eyes and took a deep breath, which sounded more like a disappointed sigh.

'Hey.' He brushed the loose strands of hair back from my face. 'What's wrong?'

I swallowed the giant lump that had lodged itself in my throat. 'I feel like an idiot. I threw myself at you, and…and…' I couldn't even get the words out. *Epic. Fail.*

He continued brushing my hair back from my forehead, smoothing it down. 'I'm sorry.'

'Just leave me.' I pressed my thighs together and clenched my fists.

He watched me with a curious expression. 'Oh hell, I can't leave you like this. Let me take care of you tonight.'

My eyes flew open and my heartbeat built to an uncomfortable rhythm. *Did he mean…?*

He peeled the blankets off me and ran his hands along my bare legs. 'Tell me how to make you come.'

I met his dark eyes, but my voice refused to cooperate. It wasn't a rejection, but it wasn't lost on me that he was refusing to share himself. For the time being, though, I was powerless to stop this. I desperately needed the release.

'What do you like, beautiful?'

My clit throbbed at his words. Oh, I wanted this. I couldn't stop now for all the money in the world. He leaned down and caressed my mouth with soft, nipping bites and tender chaste kisses.

'Touch me, please,' I begged.

He pulled back from my mouth and eased down my cotton shorts and panties, removing them completely. I should have felt embarrassed, exposed, but I didn't. I ached for his touch. He placed his palm flat against my belly, his fingers brushing past my tattoo on their way south. My breath hitched and I couldn't help but lift my hips off the bed, eager to feel his hands against me. It was like the fantasy I'd had about him, only better than I expected.

His eyes devoured me and I found myself suddenly thankful that Liz had chastised my grooming habits a few months ago and I was now in the habit of shaving completely bare. He leaned in closer and pressed a kiss against my tattooed hip and I couldn't help but let out a moan. His kisses continued all along my belly and the top of my mound. Heat and desire flooded his eyes when he pulled back to look at me.

He lifted my hips to make room for himself on the bed and sat down next to me. He leaned down to press a kiss to my belly and I let out a soft whimper.

He sat back to admire me, and ran his fingers over the clean-shaven folds. He used his thumbs to open my inner lips, gently rubbing his fingers against the wetness. 'So pretty,' he whispered.

I couldn't help but moan. My clit was swollen and overly sensitive.

'Please,' I begged.

'I'll make it better.'

He used his thumb to trace a slow, circular pattern over my clit and leaned down to kiss me. I ravaged his mouth with my tongue, so appreciative of his skilled fingers. My breathing came faster and my moans more pronounced against his onslaught of kisses. He brought his other hand up to my jaw, and tilted my head to the side, sucking and biting all along my neck while his fingers continued their mesmerizing dance.

I pressed my head back against the pillow and lifted my hips to writhe against his talented hand. I was so close. I opened my eyes to watch him and his eyes were locked on mine.

He brought his middle finger to his open mouth, and wetted it with a suckling motion. Then he gently eased his long finger inside me while continuing to work over me over with his other hand. The dual sensations were too much. I bucked my hips off the bed, matching his pace to grind against him. My moans got louder and less controlled. 'Logan,' I called out.

'Shh. I've got you, baby.' He continued sliding his finger in and out, his pace quickening just slightly as I got closer. He kissed my lips and breathed against my mouth as I came. I called out his name again and again until the last of my orgasm rocked through me.

A few moments later, I opened my eyes to see him still watching me. My cheeks were flushed and my breathing still ragged, but I didn't care how I looked just then, I only wanted to touch him, to make him feel the same way, to watch him come apart.

I sat up and reached for his waistband, working to unbutton his jeans.

'No. Just sleep now, sweetheart.' He eased my shoulders back against the bed and then adjusted his erection.

I whimpered in protest, but he kissed me once again, silencing my plea.

My eyes drifted closed and I savored his kiss.

'Just rest.'

I wanted to argue, but suddenly the bed felt too good and sleep was too close. The combined effects of the alcohol and my orgasm had left me spent. I closed my eyes and in a heartbeat the world vanished, replaced by darkness.

Chapter Five

I started awake at a thumping sound in the pitch black of my bedroom. My first thought was who the hell was knocking on my door at this hour, until I remembered Logan was sleeping in the other room.

I rose from bed and stepped across the creaky wood floors down the hall. I could see Logan crumpled on the living room floor, pounding his fists on the ground.

I sank down on the ground next to him and ran my hands up and down his back. 'It's okay. I'm here.'

He responded to my presence by gripping my hand. His knuckles were red and swollen from where he had punched the floor. He looked up at me with the most pained expression I had ever seen and my heart cinched in my chest.

'I don't want to be alone,' he murmured, bringing my hand to his lips. 'Come here.'

I curled up on my side, tucking myself into his body. He snuggled me into me like his life depended on it, clinging to me for safety. He rubbed his cheek against the top of my head, smoothing my hair down before he settled in and found a comfortable spot. Soon his breathing became deep and steady and I knew he had drifted off to sleep. I was glad my presence seemed to comfort him.

I pulled a throw blanket from the couch to cover us both and closed my eyes, concentrating on his deep, steady breaths.

At dawn the light woke us up. Well, it was either that or the aches and pains of lying on a wood floor. I rolled to my side and rubbed my aching hip.

'You didn't have to stay with me last night.' Logan's voice was thick with sleep, and even deeper than normal. I liked it. I liked that he could let his guard down with me.

'I wanted to.' I felt a sort of responsibility toward Logan. I wanted to be the one to be there for him and help him through all of this.

Without another word, he lifted me from the floor and carried me to my room, placing me carefully in the center of my mattress. He offered a small sleepy smile while still standing beside the bed.

'Stay.' I reached a hand out toward him. He looked curiously at my hand, and then at me. A moment later, he accepted my invitation. I'd been there for him last night, and now he was choosing to get closer to me, to provide me with the comfort I associated with being near him. He lay next to me and pulled me in close, holding me against his chest.

Later that morning, I woke for a second time and I crept out of bed, not wanting to wake Logan. He lay sprawled across my bed, still wearing his jeans. I admired him for a second, silently reading the words tattooed on his side. *Aut viam inveniam aut faciam tibi.* I tiptoed out of the room and sat down at the cluttered dining room table, locating my laptop under a stack of papers.

I checked my email, discovering I had two emails from Professor Clancy. The first was sent yesterday afternoon informing me that all charges against Logan had been dropped due to lack of evidence, and the possibility that the murder was committed in self-defense, and that Logan had signed himself out against the doctor's orders last night. His last line was a warning about how he and Dr. Andrews were worried that Logan might come looking for me, since he seemed to be fixated on me. A chill danced up my spine.

Clancy's second email was detailed feedback on my thesis, which apparently needed a lot more work. *Yikes*. The track changes function was in full effect, splashes of red covering nearly every inch of most of the pages. This was going to require a lot of coffee.

'That smells good.' Logan ventured into the kitchen behind me, running one hand over his hair in an attempt to smooth it down. He looked adorable first thing in the morning, sleepy-eyed and still incredibly sexy. Unfortunately, he shrugged his T-shirt on over his head, blocking my view of the delicious six-pack he sported.

I arranged two mugs on the counter and poured coffee into each. 'How do you take your coffee?'

He shrugged his shoulders. 'No clue. Surprise me.'

I laughed and added a splash of the steamed milk to each of our mugs, thankful that the elephant in the room--him getting me off last night--seemed to fade into the background. 'Did you sleep okay?'

'Yeah, that park bench set a pretty high bar.' He chuckled. 'Thank you for bringing me here. It was more than I could have expected. Thank you.' He took a sip of his coffee. 'This is good.'

I smiled and sipped my own. 'I'm glad you like it. I slept like a baby.' I shifted uncomfortably, remembering my wanton behavior last night. *Crap. Shut up, Ashlyn.*

He smirked. 'About what happened last night…' He ran a hand over his hair, hesitating to continue. I thought he'd offer some explanation for why he hadn't allowed me to touch him, to make me feel better about being such a hussy. 'That can't happen again. I appreciate everything you've done for me, but I can't put you in a compromising position. Dr. Andrews and your Professor were right and I won't do that to you. I don't want this,' he motioned between us, 'to discredit your research on amnesia.'

46

I cleared my throat, and set down my coffee mug, hoping he wouldn't notice my shaking hands. 'Of course. I was drunk and feeling sorry for myself. That won't happen again. I'm sorry.'

'Don't apologize. That was my fault as much as it was yours. I shouldn't have done that.' After a few seconds of uncomfortable silence, he set down his coffee mug, and stood. 'I guess I should get out of your way, then. I'm sure you have a lot to do.'

'Logan. Please, you don't have to go.'

'I won't take advantage of you, Ashlyn.'

I gripped his hand. 'Isn't that what I did to you last night?' I smiled, hoping to ease the tension between us.

He grinned. 'That was different. I didn't mind that at all.'

Interesting... 'I don't mind you being here either. I'd like for you to stay.'

His eyes held mine, considering the offer.

'I have a lot more work on my thesis, according to Clancy, and if you stayed here, I'd have access to ask you questions and interview you if I needed to.' It sounded halfway plausible, but truly I just didn't want to think about where he would go if he wasn't here.

'I suppose I could stay for a little while, just while you're working on your paper. If I get to be any trouble, just say the word, and I'll go.'

I nodded eagerly. *Like that would happen.* 'Great. I'm glad that's settled. Now...for breakfast...'

He sucked in a deep breath, like there was still something that didn't satisfy him. 'Ashlyn...'

'What?'

'I don't have any money, no job. Fuck, I don't even have a change of clothes. I can't take advantage of you like this. Your generosity is too much.'

'Logan, it will be okay. We'll get you what you need and when you get a job you can pay me back if it makes you feel better.'

He took a deep breath. 'Yes, I guess that will have to work.'

Logan refused breakfast, saying coffee was fine, and after a quick shower, he wanted to get out looking for work. I didn't point out that it was Sunday and he might not have much luck. He seemed eager to get out of the tiny apartment and do something productive with himself. Which was fine, since I owed Liz a phone call this morning, and I didn't want Logan to hear me lie about coming home alone last night.

I showed him the hallway linen closet where I kept the spare towels and told him he was free to use anything he wanted. I brought him into the bathroom to warn him about my rickety shower facet and how to not be inadvertently scalded.

Logan stopped in front of the bathroom mirror, and stood there seemingly mesmerized.

I stood behind him, watching as he inspected himself in the mirror. He brought his fingertips to his face, running his hand along the stubble on his jaw, tracing the line of his nose, then tilted his head to the side to see his profile. I couldn't imagine how strange it would be to not recognize your own reflection in the mirror. Things I took for granted every day, Logan was relearning.

Chapter Six

When Logan returned from an unsuccessful job search, I was only halfway through grading the essays from Clancy's graduate level psych class. He peeked around into the dining room, and asked where I kept the cleaning supplies. I showed him my pitiful collection consisting of a few random spray bottles underneath the kitchen sink. He systematically pulled each bottle from the cabinet and inspected every one.

'What are you looking for?' I asked.

'I'm going to clean the apartment. You can keep studying.'

'Logan, you don't have to do that.'

'It makes me feel useful. Like there's still something I know how to do, some way that I can contribute.'

Oh. 'Thank you. I just didn't want you to feel obligated.' I'd lived alone for a few years now, and cleaning up after myself was usually limited to the bare minimum. Still it was a far cry from how I grew up. Overflowing ashtrays and beer can pyramids had been my dad's basic style of décor. 'I know I won't be winning any awards for my housekeeping anytime soon; I just hope you don't find me disgusting.'

He laughed. 'I could never find you disgusting, Ashlyn.'

I remembered from my research that as someone with amnesia began recovering, they looked for ways to feel productive and useful. I smiled at the thought of Logan progressing into this stage.

I dug out my extra key from the junk drawer and pressed it into his palm. 'So you can come and go as you please.' Then I handed him a one-hundred-dollar bill. 'And so you can get some of the things you might need, clothes, stuff like that. Sorry I can't give you more.'

'No, this is…' He shook his head. 'Very kind of you.' We stood in the kitchen, just a foot apart, smiling at each other. 'What would I do if you hadn't come into my hospital room?'

'It's nothing, really. I enjoy having you here.'

After he cleaned the kitchen and bathroom from top to bottom, he dusted and vacuumed the entire apartment. Then I heard him banging around in the kitchen and since I was mentally unable to read another half-witted paper on theories of personality, I went to see what he was up to.

He was preparing to drop a handful of dry pasta into a pot of vigorously boiling water, but paused to smile at me. 'I hope spaghetti will be okay. That's about all I could find in the cabinets.'

'That's perfect, thank you.' I stretched my arms over my head, realizing it was already early evening. A small saucepan of tomato sauce simmered on one of the other burners, and the rich smell of tomatoes, garlic and basil teased my senses. I couldn't remember the last time someone had cooked for me.

'Sit down.' Logan led me back into the dining room. 'Let me get you a glass of wine.'

We ate at my newly cleared-off dining room table, the top of which I hadn't seen in months. The meal was delicious and after dinner neither of us was quite ready to move away from the table, so we stayed sharing the bottle of merlot.

'I was thinking more about your tattoo,' I said, swirling the crimson liquid in my glass.

He rubbed the name on his bicep. 'Logan or the Latin phrase?'

'The one in Latin, it's something an intellectual would get. Not everyone would think to get a dead language permanently inked on their body.'

'Good point. What do you think it means?'

'That you're smart. Probably college educated.'

He nodded thoughtfully; liking the direction I was headed.

'I was thinking you could take some tests online, like an IQ test, or a college placement exam. It wouldn't prove anything; it'd just give us a bit more information about you.'

'Yeah, I like that idea.'

After dinner, we settled on the couch and turned on the TV. I didn't have cable, and only got a few channels, so I opted for *Jeopardy*.

The category was *History of the 1200s*, and I was just about to change the channel when Logan leaned forward in rapt attention.

The host read the answer, 'He was the Italian philosopher and priest who died in 1274.'

'Who was Thomas Aquinas,' Logan responded without hesitation.

When the host announced that Thomas Aquinas was indeed the correct answer both of our jaws dropped open. 'You knew that.'

He nodded, his pulse racing in his neck. 'How did I know that?'

'I don't know. You're good with history?'

He held up his hand. 'Wait, he's reading the next question.' We turned our attention back to the show, and Logan answered each of the questions in that category correctly. By the time he was done, he was up on his feet, pacing the room.

'Okay, that can't be a coincidence, can it?' he asked.

'I don't think so. I couldn't have answered any of those questions. I think you've studied history pretty extensively.'

'History. Latin.' He rubbed his temples. 'Fuck,' he cursed loudly. 'I don't understand.'

I stood and crossed the room to him. 'It's okay. This is a great start. Think of what we've discovered in just the last ten minutes. We'll figure this out, I promise.'

He released a sigh and pulled me into his arms.

I nestled my head against his chest, loving the feeling of his arms around me, and his masculine scent. He seemed to crave the closeness, even if it did scare him.

'Thank you, Ashlyn.'

'For what?'

'For believing in me. For trusting me. I know I don't deserve it, this tenderness from you, but damn if I don't like it all the same.'

I couldn't explain why I trusted him so explicitly. Maybe it was the tattoo we shared, or the way I felt when I was near him. It was like I was meant to find him. But I didn't explain any of that to him. 'You're welcome,' I murmured into his chest instead.

I left early on Monday morning, after a pleasant weekend with Logan. I packed up my laptop and notebooks for a long day of grading papers for Clancy's graduate classes, administering office hours and, of course, more endless research work for my thesis since Professor Clancy had pointed out that I needed to strengthen my strategy for the sources I planned to cite.

When I returned to the apartment, exhausted and starving, it was after dark and I secretly hoped that Logan had cooked dinner again. Sadly, when I opened the apartment door, it was dark and empty inside.

I flipped on the lights and checked the table for a note. Nothing. I was curious where Logan had gone, and since he didn't have any belongings to leave behind, I had no way of knowing if he was gone for good. The thought was unnerving.

I grabbed the Chinese take-out menu from the drawer beside the fridge, and called in an order for us both.

A few minutes later, the door opened and Logan strode inside, filthy from head to toe, but looking pleased.

I was on my feet in seconds. 'Where've you been?'

'I got a job on a construction site. I'm helping to roof a building down the road.'

'That's awesome, Logan.' I playfully nudged his hip with mine. 'I was worried, though. Leave me a note next time, okay?'

'Sure.' He studied me with guarded eyes. Despite trying to keep our arrangement casual, I knew I was developing feelings for him.

'Dinner will be here in a few minutes if you want to take a shower.'

He looked down at himself in his now grungy T-shirt and jeans. 'Yeah, a shower would be great. The thing is I meant to pick up some extra clothes today, but I didn't expect to get hired so quickly, so I actually didn't have time.'

'Are you saying you don't have anything else to put on?'

'Yeah.'

My mind delved straight into the gutter with delight. 'I have some T-shirts that might fit, and I might be able to scrounge up a pair of sweats or something too.'

'Thanks, Ashlyn.' He crossed the kitchen and planted a quick kiss on my temple before heading for the bathroom.

His unexpected affection, along with his musky scent from the day spent working outside left me briefly stunned. 'Leave your clothes outside the door and I'll throw them in the wash,' I called to his retreating backside.

I heard him chuckle and stood there smiling like an idiot. We'd fallen almost too easily into a routine together, and I couldn't help but wonder what might be next. I knew for certain I didn't relish the idea of sleeping alone in my bed again tonight and wondering if Logan was okay out on the couch. I pushed the stray thoughts of Logan from my mind and went back to work.

Chapter Seven

After dinner I helped Logan make the sofa into his bed, tucking the sheet around the cushions. We had shared my bed after his nightmare, but it didn't seem like it was a good habit to get into, and Logan seemed to prefer the couch. I spread the comforter on top and added a pillow while he folded his freshly laundered jeans, shirt and boxers.

'I have to get some clothes tomorrow. I still have the money you gave me, don't worry.'

'I wasn't worried.' I smiled at him. 'But that's probably a good idea. I wouldn't recommend wearing that outfit outside the house.' I looked him up and down, making my point.

He was dressed in the largest T-shirt I owned, a women's medium from a 5k race I ran last summer. It was pink, clung to his biceps and chest and stretched only to the top of his waistband. At least the shorts seemed to fit okay. I'd stolen them from Liz after a sleepover and they no doubt had once belonged to a male. He looked down to survey himself, and placed his hands on his hips. 'What, you don't think I look good?'

'I didn't say that.' I laughed. 'Some poor girl would probably try to maul you in that form-fitting T-shirt.' *God, shut your mouth, Ashlyn.* I needed to learn to filter and not blurt out every random comment I was thinking.

He frowned just slightly, and dropped his hands from his hips. 'Actually this shirt is cutting off my circulation. I think I'll sleep without it.' He pulled it over his head and handed it back to me. 'Thanks anyway.'

'No problem. Goodnight.' I turned and fled to the safety of my room. *Was he purposely trying to torment me?*

I climbed in bed and brought the T-shirt Logan had just taken off to my nose and inhaled. It still smelled like my fabric softener. He hadn't been wearing it long enough for it to soak up any of his intoxicating scent. Which was probably for the best. I was already way more interested in him than was healthy or sane.

I lay the garment on the bed beside me and rolled over to reach into the drawer of my nightstand. If I hoped to get any sleep, I needed to relieve some of this tension. I found my vibrator rolling around in the drawer and turned it on. Its insistent buzzing seemed louder than usual and I quickly thrust it under the covers, hoping Logan wouldn't be able to hear it. I slipped it inside my panties, easing them down with my other hand. *Oh, God, that felt good.*

I lost myself in the sensation while I imagined what would happen if Logan did hear the telltale sound of my vibrator humming and came in to investigate. I wouldn't let him go this time without touching his thick cock. I bit my lip to keep from moaning as the pressure built against my clit. Just as my release started to build, Logan knocked at my bedroom door.

'Ashlyn? Are you okay?'

'Mm-hmm.' I sucked in a deep breath, the orgasm rocking through me, and pressed my lips together to keep quiet.

'I heard you call my name. Should I come in?'

'No!' I arranged the covers over my legs and flung the T-shirt from my bed. 'I mean nope. I'm good. I was just…dreaming.' *Crap!*

'Dreaming? About me?'

'Yeah, it was one of those weird, random ones that don't make any sense. But everything's fine. You can go back to bed.' *Or you could come in here and fuck me senseless.*

'Okay, if you're sure. Night, Ashlyn.'

'Night,' I grumbled.

Several hours later, I was still unable to get comfortable and turned over for the zillionth time and glanced at the clock. I'd been tossing and turning for hours. I got out of bed and headed to the kitchen for a glass of water when I heard whimpering coming from the living room. My heart thumped unevenly in my chest. Was Logan okay? I tiptoed down the hallway and into the living room. Logan was sound asleep, but his arms were thrashing around in front of his face as if he were fighting with someone in his dream.

'No, please, no,' he whispered.

He was having a nightmare. 'Logan. Logan, wake up.' I put a hand on one of his shoulders and gave him a gentle shake. He jerked away from my touch and continued mumbling incoherently.

His eyes flew open and when he saw it was me, the anguish on his face vanished. 'Oh God, Ashlyn…' He pulled me down on top of him.

'It was just a dream,' I soothed, rubbing my hands through his hair while he cradled me against his body.

It was then I noticed he was shivering. 'Logan, you're shaking.' I sat up, and moved off him.

'No. Please.' He reached for me again.

'What?'

'Lay with me.'

I nodded my consent and lay back down across his chest since there was no room beside him on the couch.

His skin felt warm to the touch but he continued to tremble. I held him until he stopped shaking and resisted the urge to ask him what he remembered from the dream. If he felt like telling me, he would. For now, I just tried to comfort him. I ran my hands along his chest and shoulders, gently massaging away his tension until he at last stopped shaking.

He patted my backside until I sat up and moved off him. 'I need paint.'

'Huh?' I rubbed my eyes, wondering if he was delirious.

'I need to paint…I saw something in my dream, and I just…I know I need to paint it. I can't explain why.'

'Okay.'

It was one in the morning. Where in the hell were we going to find an art store that was open? Nevertheless, Logan couldn't be persuaded to wait until morning, so we dressed and took the train out of downtown to a superstore that I knew was open twenty-four hours. They had a minuscule arts and crafts section, but at least we could get some paint, brushes and paper.

When we got to the checkout, I offered him my credit card. I'd gotten it only for emergencies, but I supposed needing paint at one in the morning constituted an emergency. We wouldn't be here otherwise. He scrunched his brow, but eventually took the card and swiped it to pay for his purchases.

Logan gripped the plastic bag of art supplies as if it were a rare treasure during the train ride back to my apartment. I lay my head on his shoulder and let the gentle motions of the train lull me to sleep.

When we got back to the apartment, Logan unceremoniously dumped the contents of the bag onto the dining room table. *Oh.* I hadn't realized he planned to paint tonight. He opened the package of brushes while I went into the kitchen and got him a small teacup full of water, and covered the table in paper towels.

Once he was all set up with the paints, he hugged me and told me to get some sleep. I nodded, and told him to come and get me if he needed anything. I slept with my bedroom door cracked open and listened to the sounds of him humming while he painted until I drifted off to sleep.

In the morning, Logan was gone but the remnants of his night spent painting were hard to miss. Everywhere I looked large sheets of paper covered in paint decorated much of my apartment. His paintings were dark, somber, but well done.

I wandered through my apartment like it was a museum. He'd painted several versions of a darkened warehouse, with splashes of red and moonlight leaking in through the crevices. It gave me chills just looking at it. Another was of a hand, clenched into a fist, stained with blood under the fingernails. It was surprisingly realistic. Another clue about who he was had emerged. He was an artist.

Chapter Eight

In the days that followed Logan and I fell into an easy routine together. He continued to work at the construction site each day except for the one day it rained. That day he'd returned home early with a stray cat he'd found huddled outside and a bag of dry cat food, saying that the cat was a cast-off, just like him. It broke my heart the way he compared himself to the stray, like he truly believed that no one wanted him. I couldn't say no to him after that, and that's how the damned cat, named Tom after Thomas Aquinas, came to share the apartment with us.

Having Logan living with me in such close quarters had quickly become comfortable. He was thoughtful and attentive, often doing things for me to make my day a little bit better, like having my coffee ready and small saucepan of milk simmering when I got out of bed, but a part of me ached for something that was missing. I liked his nurturing side, even if it was part of working through his amnesia and a way for him to feel like he was in some way contributing. After losing my mom at such a young age and growing up with a single father, I hadn't been pampered or taken care of that way… ever. He seemed to genuinely care, often asking about my day or how my research was coming, and he would listen thoughtfully while I answered. It was nice having him around. Being together so much meant we were now pretty much inseparable.

I found myself missing him when he was gone. I began to change my routine so that I was gone during the same hours he was, opting to study at the coffee shop or library so I didn't have to be alone in the apartment. I'd always cherished my solitude and preferred living alone, but having Logan around had altered that.

After dinner each night he'd spend a few hours online trying to piece together what little information we had about his past. He completed the IQ test and college placement exam as I suggested and did extremely well on both. He also spent time online searching through social networking sites for anyone named Logan in the Chicago area, but there were several hundred, and he couldn't find anything of interest. He also continued to help with the chores, and spent time painting after I went to bed.

After a few weeks together, and Logan's nightmares had still not let up. At first, I'd slept with my bedroom door open so I could go to him and comfort him in the night when he needed it. The last few nights though, he'd made his way into my bed and I couldn't refuse him. I wanted him close to me, too. We had quickly become inseparable--we just seemed to click together.

After takeout and watching a movie on TV, we were both exhausted from the hectic week. We went to bed together, no longer hiding under the pretense of making up the couch for him.

We crawled into my bed, covering up with the cool sheets. I sighed and closed my eyes, allowing myself to snuggle into his arms, knowing snuggling was as far as he'd take it.

I would have never thought I would feel so close to someone I'd known for such a short time. I was normally such a private person, and so careful about letting anyone in that my openness with him surprised me. I rested my hand over his heart and just enjoyed the sensation of it thumping steadily under my palm. Slowly, I drifted off to sleep in his arms.

Logan cried out in his sleep and sat up in bed.

My eyes snapped open, as I woke abruptly. 'It's okay.' I placed my hand on his shoulder, trying to calm him with gentle caresses.

His heart was pounding and his skin was damp with sweat.

'Another nightmare?'

'It was so real. I was back in that warehouse. I remember fighting with him. It felt like I really was there. Maybe everything happened like they said it did.'

'It was self-defense, right?' Who was I trying to convince, Logan or myself?

'Yeah. I think so.' He slowly nodded his head. 'That's fucked up, though. Not to know for sure.'

His doubt startled me, but I could see the pain in his eyes. I could either take a chance and trust him, or jump into accusations. I could tell he needed me to believe in him. The police had dropped all the charges, so it didn't feel right that I still doubted him. 'You're not a monster.' I snuggled into his chest, planting a kiss on his neck. 'You're sweet and gentle.'

He rubbed his knuckles across my stomach, and inched closer to me. He worked his hand lower, dipping just under the waistband of my panties. 'Logan, I don't think that's a good idea.' He'd just had a nightmare about killing a man for Christ's sake. Sex was the last thing on my mind.

He pulled his hand as though he'd been burned. 'So you are afraid of me.'

'Of course I'm not.' I brought my hand up to cup his cheek.

'Then you're disgusted with me.'

'That's not it either.' I sat up in bed, now completely awake.

He squeezed his eyes closed, as if willing the images from his nightmare to disappear as suddenly as his memory did. 'But you won't let me touch you.'

My heart pounded in my chest. I'd wanted him to touch me since his first night here. Not like this though, not because he was terrified and needing comfort.

'Logan…' I breathed.

'I need this Ashlyn. Getting lost with you chases away my demons. Let me.'

When I met his eyes, all my objections melted away. He watched me like I was something incredibly precious to him. I was stuck by the realization that if I turned him away now, I'd be validating his thoughts that he was nothing but a monster. And if I was admitting the truth, the pull between us had gotten too strong. I took his hand and placed it on my chest, letting him feel the pounding of my heart. His eyes widened momentarily, as he felt its insistent thumping. My body wanted nothing more than his touch, but because I'd just refused him a second before, I didn't know what to say.

'Logan.' His name slipped from my lips and it was all that needed to be said.

He lowered me to the pillow once again, and pinned me to the bed, kissing and nuzzling my neck. His stubble scratched against my skin and I inhaled the scent of his aftershave, trying to memorize this moment.

He hauled me up to a sitting position and removed my shirt, throwing it to the floor. I liked that he didn't ask; he just did what he wanted, all with perfect skill. His gaze lowered to my chest, and his hands joined the inspection, softly running his fingertips along the bottom swells of my breasts, dipping between my cleavage, circling my nipples, but never touching them.

Heat and dampness flooded between my legs and I released a small whimper.

'Shh. I'll make it better,' he whispered.

He lowered his head and kissed my breasts in the same pattern, everywhere but where I needed him. When my panting grew heavier, he finally slid his tongue across one nipple and I arched my back, pressing my breasts forward into his mouth. His tongue lapped slow, easy circles while he pushed my breasts together with his hands. I'd never had so much attention paid to my breasts before, and never knew it would make me so hot.

I snaked my hands underneath his shirt, and ran my hands across his abs, loving the solid feel of him. I hauled his shirt over his head and it joined mine on the floor. He continued kissing me and the effect of his skin, warm and soft, against mine drove me over the edge. I wrapped my legs around his waist and thrust my hips into his, grinding against him. I released a strangled cry at the contact.

After kissing me for several minutes more while I continued to grind against him, he reached between us and pushed my panties down my thighs. Thank God. I was ready. I reached for his waistband, but he shook his head. 'Not yet.'

I swallowed and placed my hands by my sides, nodding like a good girl. I didn't want to do anything to drive him away. Not when I so badly needed the release he could give me. 'Logan,' I moaned loudly, frustration and sexual tension evident in my voice.

'I know, baby.' He kissed my forehead and lowered himself to his elbows, positioning himself between my legs. He pulled my legs apart suddenly, and held them there. I was completely exposed, and on display for his inspection, but I didn't feel self-conscious in that moment. I wanted everything he could give me.

Just like that first night, he spread me open, sliding his fingers up and down the length of my wetness. I loved how unrushed he was. With the two other men I'd had as lovers, it'd been a sprint to the finish line. They'd hurried to get inside me, to get off and then get out. Logan only seemed concerned with drawing out my pleasure, like the act of loving me could heal him in some small way.

63

After several minutes of torturing me with his fingers and watching me squirm while he kissed my inner thighs, belly, and hips, he finally flicked his tongue across my clit. My hips shot straight off the bed. He chuckled and held my thighs in place, then lowered his mouth to me once again. He suckled my clit into his mouth, his tongue doing laps against me. I panted and cursed, and thrust against his mouth, long past caring about how I looked to him. He made me hotter than I'd ever been.

He pulled my legs apart and eagerly suckled at my folds. I cried out loudly. There was nothing tentative or shy about his touches. He worked me over as if he'd known my body for years rather than weeks. Seeing this side of him was new discovery. There was nothing fleeting or impersonal about his lovemaking. With Logan it was all or nothing. *Was that why he had held himself back from making love to me?*

When my cries grew louder, he still didn't relent. He only held me in place and continued to lick and suck on my most sensitive parts until I fell apart. My orgasm built slowly, but once it crashed through me, I moaned his name in a final whimper and fell back against the bed, completely spent.

Logan chuckled at me, and curled his body against mine, holding me while the aftershocks of my orgasm pulsed through me.

After a little while, he found my panties and slid them up my legs, securing them in place and then folded me into his arms again. Playtime was apparently over.

I hated feeling like I was using him for my own pleasure, but I knew he wouldn't let me return the favor. I didn't have the energy to examine this new part of our relationship the way I wanted to, but my last thought before I drifted off to sleep was that if this was the only way I could provide comfort to him and chase away his nightmares, then so be it. *Selfless, I know. Mother-friggin-Teresa, right here.*

Chapter Nine

Saturdays at noon was my standing coffee date with Liz, and as I strolled into our usual coffee shop, I picked at the cat hair on my black sweater. 'Damn cat,' I muttered.

'You got a cat? Since when?' Liz said, coming up behind me.

'Oh, um, yeah. I got a cat this week.'

She eyed me curiously. 'O-kay. But you hate cats.'

'I don't *hate* cats.' I actually did hate them.

'Whatever.' She rolled her eyes.

We ordered our coffee and claimed the lounge chairs in the back. Liz's eyes were on me from the second I sat down. 'What?'

She cocked her head. 'Something's going on with you.' She took a quick sip of her bucket-sized iced Americano, biting into the straw.

I tried to act casual, but crap, once Liz was on the trail, there was no hiding anything you didn't want her to know.

'Something's not adding up. You're done working with Logan, Professor Clancy told me he's no longer at the hospital and you've still been bailing on coffee. . And you've got to admit the cat is strange.'

I removed the lid from my latte, needing something to do with my hands. 'Nope, nothing' going on. Clancy returned my thesis with tons of edits, so I've just been busy working on that. And the cat…that's nothing. He was just a stray I found.'

She narrowed her eyes at me. 'Are you kidding me? You think it's your job to fix all the stray men and animals in the city of Chicago? Honey…' She shook her head. 'You've got to let this go.'

I took another sip of my drink, trying to think of a way to change the subject. Liz had a history of drawing truths out of me that she didn't need to know about. Such as my grooming habits, or the fact that I didn't own any sex toys, which we promptly changed with a trip to the sex shop several months ago. Not that I regretted that particular intervention, but still, wasn't I entitled to some privacy?

Besides she would flip if she found out Logan was living with me. If she told Clancy or anyone else, I didn't want to think about what might become of my grant to study amnesia patients. Surely this was crossing some sort of line. At least we hadn't had sex. God, if someone thought I was trading sexual favors for academic research… I shivered.

Liz noticed, narrowing her eyes at me. 'Wait a second.' She lifted her finger into the air. 'Uh-uh, no. No way.'

'What?' My stomach clenched with nerves.

'You're still in contact with him, aren't you?'

'Who?'

'Don't play dumb. You know I'm talking about Logan. You must still be talking to him; otherwise you'd be more upset or blabbering about him nonstop.'

'Maybe.'

'Girl, you better spill right now.'

'Stop, Liz.' I looked down into my drink. 'There's nothing to tell.' Other than that I was lusting badly for a sick, possibility violent man with a past neither of us knew a lick about. *Oh, just that.*

She narrowed her eyes, but thankfully let it drop.

After Liz and I chatted for a little while longer, she insisted on driving me home, saying she wanted to meet my cat. No matter what I tried to tell her, that I'd prefer to walk, or that I was going to stop at the library on my way, she continued to insist, to the point where I knew if I kept making up excuses, she'd get suspicious. I finally relented.

'What's his name anyways?'

'Who?'

'Your cat.'

'Oh, um, Tom.'

'Tom?' she questioned with a smirk. 'You're even more in need of a man than I realized.'

We rode in silence to my apartment, and I prayed all the while that Logan would be out. He didn't work on Saturdays, but if there was a God, I prayed he'd grant my request.

When I unlocked the door to my apartment and pushed it open, I breathed a sigh of relief. Everything was still and silent. Thank God. Logan wasn't here.

'Here Tommy boy,' Liz snickered. She loved cats and had two of her own, which I'd always complained about, making the fact that I had a cat all the more unbelievable.

Oh crap, the paintings. Unless I could convince Liz I'd suddenly taken up painting, as soon as she entered the dining room, I was fucked. And since she knew I didn't have an artistic bone in my body, the jig was up.

'Well hello there, Thomas.' I heard Liz talking from the other room. 'You're a pretty kitty.' I walked back into the living room. Maybe I could just keep her in this room. Thank God for that damn cat.

'Yep. That's him, the new man in my life.' I smiled. He was a cute cat I had to admit. He was soft-gray and white. The best part about him was that he didn't use a litter box, he scratched at the door when he needed out so there was no mess to clean up.

She sat the cat down at her feet. 'I'm just going to use the bathroom before I head out. Too much coffee.'

''Kay.'

I breathed a sigh of relief the moment she disappeared down the hall. Maybe I could pull this off.

A second later, Liz burst down the hallway. 'Call the police!'

'What? Why?'

'There's a man masturbating in your bathroom!' She grabbed an umbrella from the foyer and held it in front of her like a weapon, poised for battle. 'Ashlyn! Did you hear what I said? Call the police!'

I swallowed my pride. 'Logan? You'd better come out here,' I called down the hallway.

Liz's eyes widened in shock. 'Lo-Logan?'

He emerged from the hall a second later, a white towel draped around his hips, his chest still damp and glistening with water droplets from the shower. His cheeks were flushed and I suddenly remembered Liz's claim that he had been masturbating. I filed that mental image away to inspect later.

'What the fuck is he doing here?' Liz shouted, motioning to Logan.

Logan looked uncomfortable and ashamed. A protective urge swelled up inside me. No one was going to make him feel bad for being here. 'Liz, chill. I'll explain. Logan, why don't you go in my room and get dressed?'

He disappeared down the hall without another word.

'What the hell's the matter with you?' Liz whispered loudly as soon as he was gone.

I held up my hand, stopping her mid-rant. 'It's not what you think. He's just staying here until he gets on his feet. And there's nothing going on between us.'

'Right. And that's why he's jacking off in your bathroom, because nothing's going on?'

'Yes. Exactly. He's not getting any action from me. I know it sounds crazy to you, but he's my friend.'

She took a deep breath and closed her eyes. When she reopened them, she seemed a little more relaxed. 'You're lucky I love you, girl, because otherwise, I would be calling the police.'

'Thanks, Lizzie, but you can't tell anyone about this. Especially not Clancy.'

'Obviously,' she scoffed. 'At least you do still have some sense of right and wrong.'

I removed the umbrella from her hands. 'Drop the weapon. I promise he's nice.'

Logan emerged a few minutes later, dressed in jeans and a worn gray T-shirt.

'Hey, I'm Logan.' He extended a hand to Liz. I smiled at him warmly, thankful that despite this awkward situation, he was polite and well mannered.

Liz smiled at him too, seeming to notice for the first time how attractive he was. I'd seen that smile before, and it was usually reserved for a man she was trying to impress. 'Nice to meet you.' She grinned.

'And I see you've met Tom?' Logan looked down at the cat who had snaked himself around Liz's ankles.

'Ah. Now it makes sense. Tom is your doing.'

He nodded and bent to pick up the cat, holding him against his chest. 'Yeah.'

'Ashlyn hates cats,' Liz remarked.

'You hate cats?' Logan asked, turning to me with a look of concern.

'I don't *hate* them.'

Logan turned to Liz for the truth, already aware that within thirty seconds of meeting her, she was not one to hold back. 'She hates them. Which means she must *really* like you.'

Logan smiled at me warmly. 'Go outside, Thomas.' Logan walked the cat to the door and herded him outside.

Liz stayed most of the afternoon to chat with Logan and me. We shared a glass of wine and I turned on some music, the blues that seemed to speak to Logan, but had yet to spark a memory. I was relieved to see Liz was polite to him, even though I could tell she'd voice everything that was really on her mind later.

When she was ready to leave, she asked me to walk her out, which was code for *I'm going to pump you for information out of your company's earshot.*

Great. I slid on my shoes and followed her into the hall. She stayed quiet as we descended the stairs, but I could tell her wheels were turning. That only frightened me more.

Once we reached the street, we stopped in front of her car. 'So there's really nothing going on between you and Logan?'

I nodded my head.

'Prove it to me.'

I cocked my head, trying to understand. Did she want to inspect my lady parts for signs of entry? 'How?'

'Like for instance…if I set you up on a date, you'll go?'

Oh crap. 'Of course.'

She took a deep breath, obviously pleased with herself. 'Great. It's tomorrow night. Eight o'clock with Jason, the guy you met at the club. He's been asking about you.'

She had this set up all along, that sneak! I opened my mouth to protest, when Liz patted the top of my head.

'And wear a dress.'

She hopped into her car and drove away.

Chapter Ten

That night sounds of incoherent mumbling woke me from a deep sleep. It took me a moment to realize Logan was having another nightmare. I heard him gasp and shot straight up in bed. He thrashed his arms and legs, and his breaths coming in heavy gasps.

'Logan,' he mumbled. 'No, Logan...'

Logan?

I shook his shoulders, trying to pull him from his nightmare. 'Wake up, Logan, wake up.' I continued to grip his shoulders and when I happened to glance down s, I noticed he had an erection.

His eyes opened and he let out a gasp once he saw it was me hovering over him.

'Are you okay?

He nodded, still staring up at me.

'What was the dream about?'

He closed his eyes just briefly then opened them again. 'I don't remember.'

For the first time, I didn't know if I could believe him. Nightmares that vivid weren't easily forgotten. I had the nagging feeling that he was keeping something from me. I felt certain that he had identified the Logan from his tattoo in his dream, and now I was half-afraid of finding out the mystery Logan's identity.

Maybe it had been a bad idea to start calling the man beside me by that name. It clearly belonged to someone else.

'Are you sure you're okay?' I asked. I didn't want to tell him that he had called out the name Logan any more than he wanted to admit to me what he had been dreaming about.

His breathing had returned to normal. 'I'm fine. It wasn't a nightmare this time.'

Oh. I see. 'Okay. Goodnight then.'

'Night.' He curled onto his side, facing away from me.

I hugged my pillow against my chest, feeling for the first time that I truly was sharing my bed with a stranger.

The next morning neither of us spoke about last night's dream, but it weighed heavily on my mind as I made our coffee. The dream had turned him on sexually, and he'd called out the name Logan. I knew I was developing real feelings for him, and I was beginning to suspect that this wouldn't end well for us. There couldn't be a happily ever after for someone who didn't even know who they were.

I poured myself a cup of coffee and heard Logan get up and head into the shower. His new job was starting today. Having finished with the roofing job that had kept him busy over the past few weeks, he'd secured a job painting a mural on one of the buildings being made over as part of the renovation process. With his earnings from the construction job, he'd bought more clothes, and a nicer set of paints and brushes. His wardrobe now consisted of a few pairs of jeans, boxer briefs, socks and T-shirts.

Other than the nightmares, he was an easy houseguest to have around. He was neat and tidy, and did more than his fair share of the chores. Once he realized that I either skipped dinner altogether or ate a cup of instant noodles after arriving home, he also began cooking dinner for us. Some nights he'd call for takeout so at least we could sit down and eat together.

In other ways though, I could tell he wasn't entirely comfortable living here. Every day he packed up his toiletries from the bathroom, his shaving cream, razor and toothbrush, putting them in the backpack in which he kept his belongings. I told him several times he could leave his things in the bathroom, since I was certainly no neat freak. A few extra things left out wouldn't have bothered me, not to mention I'd come to enjoy the smell of his shaving cream and aftershave in the steam-filled bathroom after his shower. I had even cleared out a spot in the drawer, but he seemed content with packing them up every day, like he didn't really live here, but was only staying temporarily.

We never talked about him moving out and that was just fine with me. I had a feeling that without him and Tom my apartment would feel empty and depressing.

I pulled on my black shift dress, and slipped on a pair of heels. Giving myself one more glance in the mirror to be sure my makeup and hair were in place, I headed out to the living room.

Logan was sitting on the couch with my laptop balanced across his lap. He looked up at the sound of my heels clicking against the wood floor.

'Wow. You look nice. Where are you headed?'

'Thanks,' I mumbled, looking down. 'I have a date tonight.'

'A date?' His face betrayed his confusion and another emotion I couldn't quite identify...jealousy?

'Liz set me up,' I explained.

He nodded, regaining his composure.

'Will you zip up my dress?' I turned my back to him.

His fingers against my bare back as he slid the zipper up the dress shouldn't have excited me the way they did. Maybe this date would be good for me. I needed to stop fixating on Logan. Especially since it was clear he wasn't interested in an actual emotional connection with me.

I grabbed my purse, and Logan went back to the computer, not looking up at me again as I gathered my things and headed out.

The date wasn't as bad as I'd expected. Jason was nice, but something just felt wrong about dating someone who was still an undergrad. *Rob the cradle, much?* I knew Liz never had a problem with dating younger men, and that I looked young for my age so I shouldn't either. But he was only twenty-two and more interested in keg parties than discussing world issues. I did my best to maintain the conversation, chatting casually with him throughout dinner, and the three glasses of wine I drank certainly helped to loosen me up.

After dinner he walked me to my apartment, and when he kissed my hand in the street and asked if he could come up, I could only nod. I was damn curious about how Logan might respond to me bringing a man home. If that was jealousy I'd caught a hint of before, perhaps seeing another man interested in me would force him to face his feelings for me. It might not have been the best plan, but with three glasses of Chardonnay down, my reasoning was shot. I lead Jason up the stairs and unlocked the door, my heart pounding in my chest.

I expected Logan to be sitting at the dining room table painting like he did every night, but the apartment was silent and dark. *Oh.* My anticipation died down and was replaced with a sense of dread. I now had an eager man who I wanted nothing to do with in my apartment and Logan wasn't even here. That or he was in my room sleeping, but it wasn't even eleven yet. He never went to bed this early.

I flipped on a lamp, and asked Jason to wait for me in the living room. I poured another glass of wine for each of us before I settled on the couch. We continued chatting for a little while, but when I saw him focusing in on my mouth as I spoke, I knew he intended to kiss me. I held my wine in front of me like a shield, hoping it would provide a buffer. But Jason knew what he was doing. He took the glass from my hands and set it on the coffee table. When he leaned in toward me I was too stunned to do anything but close my eyes and let him press his lips to mine. The kiss was nice, but I felt nothing, no spark, no passion like I did with Logan. I put my hands on his chest and pushed him back, breaking the kiss.

'Ashlyn?' Logan's groggy voice came from behind me.

Jason leapt to his feet at the sight of Logan, shirtless, tattooed and looking angry.

I jumped from the couch, and placed a palm on Logan's chest as a silent apology, or just for the chance to touch him, I didn't know. He nudged my hand out of the way, and stepped closer, still staring Jason down.

'Logan, stop.' I gripped his chest again, silently chastising his macho behavior. 'Jason, I think you'd better go. Thanks for dinner.'

'Yeah,' he said without another glance in my direction and stormed from the apartment.

Once the door closed, I realized how utterly tense the situation felt. I was standing only inches from Logan, my palm still pressed to his chest, which was rapidly rising and falling with each quick breath. Our eyes locked and I could read the hurt and anger in those depths as clear as day. He looked down at my hand still pressed over his heart and let his eyes fall closed. When he reopened them a moment later, his anger was replaced with something else entirely…desire.

'Tell me why you're angry,' I prodded gently.

'I can't.' His words were clipped and tight.

I took a deep breath, and summoned my courage. We couldn't keep sidestepping around each other in this tiny apartment. Not anymore. 'Damn it, Logan. Stop holding back. I know you feel something for me.' All my cards were on the table now, my heart thumping while I waited to hear his response.

'Ashlyn,' he pleaded, his voice cracking. 'I can't do this…'

'Why?' I challenged. I knew damn well the reasons why we weren't supposed to be together, but I wanted to hear his version. Then I could poke holes in his argument. I was tired of my neat, orderly life, of never stepping out of line. Not to mention, the wine I'd had earlier had provided some much needed liquid courage.

He released a slow breath, stalling for more time. 'I've tried to hold part of myself back from you, to not get emotionally attached in case I woke up one day and I remembered I had a wife and three kids at home.'

Ouch, that stung. I stared up at him wondering where we'd go from here. If I was the sane and logical person I'd always claimed to be, I'd walk away, end this charade now. But of course I couldn't. It was too late, and I was in too deep for that.

Logan raked a hand through his hair. 'And I thought that if I didn't let you touch me, I wouldn't be as involved, but I was wrong. Bringing you pleasure, seeing how responsive you are to me, watching you come.' He closed his eyes, gathering his thoughts. 'You're beautiful, Ashlyn, and smart, and sweet. It's impossible to be here with you and not develop feelings for you. But I won't let myself hurt you.'

My chest felt tight, and I swallowed thickly. 'I'd rather be hurt all at once for a specific reason, than be hurt slowly every day.'

'Don't.' He frowned, but his eyes softened just enough for me to see that his resolve was falling away.

'You kicked my date out.' I pouted, even though I wasn't the least bit sorry to see Jason go. That doesn't mean that Logan shouldn't feel bad.

'Fuck,' he groaned. 'I'm done fighting myself. And my willpower is shot after seeing you with that tool.' He shook his head.

I let my hand trail down his side, tracing the script over his ribcage as I caressed him. He exhaled heavily. When I reached his hips, and the waistband of his shorts, he reached for my hand to stop me, his eyes pleading with mine in a silent battle. He wanted me to continue, but he thought the right thing to do was to stop. Screw right and wrong. I knew what I wanted, what I needed. *Logan.*

I shook my head slowly. 'Let me.'

His hand fell away from mine, and relief crossed his face. I stroked his growing erection through the gym shorts and his lips parted to suck in a quick breath. Maybe this was what I needed to do with him all along--take control so that he didn't have to stop to think about what we were doing. He gripped my wrist, holding my hand in place, not allowing me to move, but also not pushing me away.

It was official--I'd lost all cognitive thought, all sense of reason. There was only Logan. I wanted to please him, to taste every inch of his skin and hear his dirty endearments at the pleasure my mouth could provide. He turned on something strange and exciting inside me. Something dark that I knew I shouldn't explore, yet felt compelled to discover. I'd played it safe for too damn long. I wanted to experience this man. Common sense be damned.

I began to ease the shorts down over his hips, but he lifted my chin and shook his head. He pressed a quick kiss to my mouth and whispered, 'Not yet. I want to make you come first.'

Oh, not again. I was bound and determined to drive him insane with pleasure, and as difficult as his offer was to refuse, I shook my head. 'Not this time...'

I dropped to my knees on the floor and tugged his shorts down so that his erection sprang free. Everything about this man was gorgeous, even his cock was beautiful. It was thicker and longer than any I'd seen before and was as hard as a rock. A drop of fluid glistened on the head and I brought my tongue forward to taste it. He groaned at the sensation.

I'd never particularly enjoyed giving blowjobs before, but with Logan I wanted to taste and savor every inch and arouse every response of pleasure I could. I flicked my tongue back and forth, teasing him. He groaned and gripped his cock in one hand, and stroked my jaw with the other. 'Open,' he commanded.

A rush of wetness dampened my panties at his tone. I loved it when he took charge. I met his eyes and obeyed, opening as wide as I could while he eased himself forward into my mouth. The image of his fist gripping his cock as he slid it in and out of my mouth made me moan each time he retreated. I gripped his thighs, running my nails against his skin. His muscles were tensed and tight with the effort of holding himself steady. I continued sucking him into my mouth, while letting my hands explore his stomach, his ass, cupping his firm sack.

I closed my hand around his and began stroking the length of his shaft while he watched my mouth and tongue lap circles around the sensitive head. He fed his length into my mouth, and sucked in a hiss. 'Oh, fuck,' he breathed, heavily. I must have made a noise because his gaze collided with mine. 'That's right, baby.'

His pace increased and his breathing grew heavier. My jaw ached, but I didn't dare stop now. Suddenly he withdrew from my mouth, his unexpected retreat causing a loud suckling sound. I looked up at him, his cock hard and damp with my saliva.

'Come here,' he growled, hauling me to my feet. He pressed several soft kisses against my damp swollen lips, his way of thanking me for the oral affection. I smiled at him like a schoolgirl proud of her test score. He reached behind me to unzip my dress, and I helped him pull it down so I could step out of it.

I stood before him in a pair of black lace panties and a matching bra. His hands skidded down my sides, past my hips and gripped my ass, hauling me against him.

He pulled up his shorts and I was about to protest, when he took my hand and led me into the bedroom. The mental image of him trying to walk to my room with his shorts around his ankles made me smile.

When we reached the bed, he unclasped my bra and pulled it from my shoulders, lovingly stroking me with his fingertips as he did. Then he bent down and lowered my panties until they dropped to the floor and I could step out of them. He kissed and nuzzled my neck and collarbone, while his hands caressed my backside.

I kissed him for a few minutes more, and then lowered myself to the bed, tugging him down along with me. I pulled him on top of me until his body hovered over mine, and wrapped my legs around his back. I locked my ankles together and pulled him in close.

I ground against him while trying to tug his shorts down. His breathing accelerated and his mouth hovered just over mine. 'Ashlyn, are you sure?'

'I want you, Logan.' I kissed him again. Hard.

A broken plea fell from his lips. 'Because if you have any doubts…we need to stop now.'

'Please don't,' I said. He stilled.

'I meant please don't stop, Logan.'

That had a profound effect on him. He pushed his shorts down over his hips, his freed cock heavily resting against my belly. I snaked my hand between our bodies and stroked him.

He groaned and looked down at me with wonder while I continued my long, easy strokes. 'Ashlyn, I need to be inside you,' he murmured, peppering my mouth with kisses.

'Yes,' I whispered.

He pulled back and lifted himself off of me. 'Do you have protection?'

I hadn't thought about that. I shook my head. I hadn't had a use for condoms since I never really dated.

He closed his eyes. 'It's not you. I just…I don't know where *I've* been.'

Oh. 'Logan. I read in your file, they tested you for all kinds of things. You're clean.' *Way to kill the romance, Ashlyn.*

He breathed a sigh of relief. 'That's…good, right?'

I kissed his lips. 'That's very good, because so am I. And I'm also on the pill.' I'd been taking it for years to regulate my erratic periods.

Nothing stood between us now except for the butterflies that danced in my stomach. I didn't want to examine too closely what this act of intimacy between us might mean. I knew what we were about to do would deepen my connection to Logan. I wasn't sure what it might mean, or *not mean* to him. His lack of availability terrified me and I was beginning to dread the day he remembered his former life. Would he still be here with me?

'Hey, are you okay?' He noticed my distraction and kissed my temple.

'Yes,' I answered, masking my insecurity. I knew it was selfish to want to keep him with me, especially if it turned out he had loved ones waiting for him, but that wouldn't stop me from enjoying him while I could.

He brushed a strand of my hair back from my face, and stared into my eyes. The dim moonlight restricted my view, but I could see just enough of him. The green flecks in his eyes, his firm, muscled chest, the ink over his ribs, the flat plain of his stomach, and his impressive cock. I let my eyes drift closed, and savored his attention. I relaxed into the moment and attempted to commit this to memory.

Logan had other ideas. He moved down my body, kissing his way across my chest, my stomach, my hips… then he stopped. I rose up on my elbows and looked down. He met my eyes and smiled. 'I want you to watch me get you off. You're beautiful when you come.'

My cheeks flushed. *Crap!* What did I look like when I came? Then his tongue slid across me and I forgot about being self-conscious. I watched as he used broad strokes to gently lap against me. The sensation coupled with the visual was overwhelming. I let out a soft murmur and shifted, trying to get closer. He brought his hands to my hips and pulled me in closer to his face, then held me in place while he maintained his lazy pace, his tongue providing the most exquisite torture as he licked, suckled, and nipped at my sensitive clit.

I squeezed my eyes closed and let my head fall back, concentrating on the sensations.

Logan stopped suddenly. 'Open them. Open your eyes.'

I looked down at him and he once again started his slow torture, licking his warm tongue up the length of my wetness. His pace increased and so did my panting. It had never been like this for me before. I felt like I could come undone and never again come down from my high.

Much more of this and I was going to reach my peak. 'Logan,' I called out.

His eyes lifted to watch me. His attention didn't let up, his mouth creating a gentle suction against me, and a few seconds later I was panting and writhing even more frantically against him. He held me in place, his eyes locked on mine.

I exploded into a million pieces, calling out his name over and over again. I collapsed back onto the pillow as Logan kissed his way up my body. When he reached my mouth, he was smiling. 'Beautiful girl, let me fuck you now.'

'Yes,' I moaned, reaching for his cock. He was still hard as steel and ready for me.

He lay down on the bed beside me and pulled me on top of him until I was straddling him.

Oh. This wasn't really the position I'd had in mind. I wasn't good at being the one in control, and he was by far the largest man I'd been with, so I wasn't entirely sure how this position was going to work. I sat across his hips, facing him while he nuzzled against my breasts and kissed me.

He gripped my hips, and lifted me up, positioning the head of his cock at my opening. He slid himself against my wetness, preparing his cock to slide inside me. I groaned at the sensation.

I was about to beg when he finally eased the head several inches inside me. I felt stretched to capacity and I gasped at the fullness. 'Logan, ah…'

He groaned deeply, his masculine tone rumbling through me. 'Too much, baby?'

'Yeah,' I moaned.

'Fuck, you're tight.' He pulled out just a bit.

His voice shot a pulse of desire through me. I wanted more. I wanted to be completely filled up by him and hear him curse and moan at the pleasure of being inside me. He lifted me up off his cock so just the tip was still inside me, and allowed me to get used to his size. Then he pushed himself up, sinking several inches into me once again.

I sucked in a breath and held it.

'Christ, Ashlyn,' he growled, 'are you sure this is okay?'

I nodded tightly, needing to concentrate.

'Breathe, baby.' He lifted my hips off him, easing the sensation just a little. 'I feel like I'm hurting you.'

I sucked in a deep breath at his command. 'No.' I gazed down at him, and ran my hands over his chest. 'I like it…you're just…big.'

He grinned, a cocky half smile. 'But you like it?'

'Yeah,' I breathed.

He thrust into me carefully, pushing in and then withdrawing with an easy rhythm. His breathing was rough and heavy as if the act of holding back was torturous for him. Once seated deep inside, he pulled me down across his chest and held me, kissing my lips in between his gentle thrusts. 'You feel so fucking good, baby.'

'Logan,' I groaned.

He responded with a groan of his own. 'Can you handle more, sweetheart?'

More? He wasn't all the way in yet? I nodded, rubbing my cheek against his.

He held me in place while he pushed in farther. His eyes drifted closed with pleasure as he sunk all the way into me. I whimpered with a mix of pleasure and pain as he secured me over the top of him and thrust into me at a faster pace.

My whimpers grew louder and his breaths came in heavy pants against my neck. I felt so close to him just then, with the smell of his aftershave intoxicating me and his rough stubble brushing against my neck. It was the most intimate act we could share.

He brushed his fingertips over my cheek and met my eyes in a tender moment. 'Are you sure you're okay?'

'Yeah. I love it.'

He smiled. 'Good. Because I love being inside you.' He kissed me once more and in one smooth motion, rolled us over on the bed so that I was underneath him.

I held tight to his straining biceps while he sunk slowly into me. Now that I was used to his size, I loved the way it made me feel. Incredibly at his mercy. *His.*

I arched against him, squeezing my eyes closed and exposing my neck. He dampened my throat with wet kisses and began fucking me harder. Each time he thrust into me, I lifted to meet him. Soon his grunts mingled with mine and we lost ourselves entirely.

He wasn't overly vocal during sex, but I loved the sound of his heavy breathing and soft grunts near my ear. 'I'm going to come,' he whispered, clutching my hips tightly. He thrust a final few times before his warm semen spilled inside me.

He kissed my mouth gently and lay down beside me. 'You are amazing.' He smiled.

'So are you,' I whispered. I nestled into Logan's arms with my back against his front. He cuddled around me. I'd never felt so happy and alive. Logan, with no memory of his own life was teaching me how to live in the moment and enjoy mine.

Chapter Eleven

When I woke a few hours later, groggy from the wine and the uncomfortable position I'd fallen asleep in, it took me a moment to recall what had happened earlier. As the memories of making love to Logan danced through my memory, a smile pulled at my lips. Despite the fact that going on a date with one man and making love to another within the span of a few hours was sort of sleazy, it was a great night. And if the little bit of soreness deep within my body was any indication, he'd probably enjoyed it too.

I rolled over to cuddle with Logan, but I realized I was in the bed alone. I'd thought that last night's sex has brought us closer and revealed a new side of him to me, but he was already gone.

I was still naked, so I pulled on a tank top and a pair of panties and wandered out of the bedroom to find him.

He was sitting at the dining room table, shirtless and hunched over a nearly-finished painting.

I ran my hand along his back, not expecting him to startle at my touch.

'Hey.' He glanced up quickly, but then continued to work, the brush moving quickly in his hand.

Hurt over his less-than-warm greeting after just fucking me and leaving me in bed alone, I gazed down at the painting that was capturing his attention.

It was a beautiful woman with dark flowing hair. Her hair was swept over one shoulder, with the smallest hint of a grin on her full lips. Her eyes were chocolate brown, and her skin had the hint of an olive complexion. She looked exotic and alluring and even more than that, Logan had captured her sensual essence. Instead of admiring what a talented artist he was, I felt jealous. Who was the woman in the painting?

I went to the kitchen to get a glass of water and allowed Logan to finish his painting. When I returned to the dining room, he was rinsing his brushes.

'Why'd you get up? Did you have a nightmare?'

He shook his head. 'I didn't fall asleep.'

Oh. I felt embarrassed that after our lovemaking I'd passed out, exhausted.

'I remembered something.'

'That's great, Logan,' I tried to sound encouraging.

'I don't think you're going to like it.'

'Why not? What was it?' I mentally braced myself.

'A woman.'

'Her?' I motioned to the painting.

He nodded. 'When I was inside you…I remembered a woman from my past. I'm sorry, I know it sounds… crazy, but I had to paint her to see if I could remember anything else.'

My stomach twisted into a painful knot. *While he was inside of me?* I felt faint. *Breathe, Ashlyn.* 'And did you?'

'No.' He shook his head. 'I'm sorry; I didn't mean to upset you.' His eyes held mine, looking concerned.

'Logan, it's okay. I know you had a life before me and that you want to piece it all together.'

'I'm beginning to doubt I'll ever remember.'

'You will,' I said confidently. He'd made such great progress already and it had only been a couple of weeks. *I'm just scared what's going to happen to us when you remember it*, I added silently.

86

Chapter Twelve

By the morning there were three more paintings of the woman. I toured the dining room, examining his new artwork. In one, the mysterious femme fatale was sipping a glass of red wine, in another she wore a yellow sundress and in the third... Well, the third painting just pissed me off. She was lying in bed with only a white sheet covering her, early morning light illuminating her dewy skin. Logan had perfectly captured the dips and curves of her enviable body. It took great restraint not to throw that painting through the open window.

I'd been so set on helping him to remember his former life, but now I only wanted him to forget his past and build a future with me. I knew it was a dangerous way to think and would only lead to heartbreak, but I couldn't help that I was falling for him.

I worked on cleaning up my thesis all morning and then late that afternoon, I heard Logan finally arrive home from work. He'd been planning out and sketching his mural before the actual painting was set to begin in a week or so.

He found me sitting at the table, laptop forgotten, lost in thought as I stared at the much-hated painting of the woman lying in bed. He came up behind me and kneaded my shoulders. 'Hey there. You need a break?'

'Hm?' I mumbled, looking up into his beautiful hazel eyes. 'What'd you have in mind?'

He bent down and kissed my temple. I couldn't help but wonder if he was being sweet to me to make up for turning me away last night to paint another woman. I reminded myself that it wasn't his fault and let myself enjoy the moment, the sensation of his strong hands massaging my shoulders, and the feel of his warm breath on the back of my neck.

'That feels nice,' I murmured, reaching around behind me to grip his waist.

I hauled him against me and could feel that he was already hard.

He continued the massage for a few minutes more and then lifted me from the chair, held me against his chest and carried me to the bedroom. Once we reached my room, with Tom right on our heels, he set my feet on the floor and maneuvered Tom into the hallway before shutting the door.

He stood there, watching me.

'What?' I asked, reaching for him.

'I missed you today.' He nuzzled against my neck and left a trail of soft, damp kisses.

His admission shocked me. I had assumed I was alone in the feelings I was developing for him. When his mouth met mine, our kiss turned frantic. Our lips connected, our tongues each desperately stroking the other.

I groaned. 'Logan. I need you.'

He unbuttoned my jeans, thrust them down to my ankles and helped me pull them off. He pushed me back against the wall, holding me in place while he assaulted my mouth with kisses. His hand snaked between us and stroked me until I was wet and ready. Before I had to beg, he pulled his jeans and boxers down just enough to free himself and then lifted me up, using the wall as leverage to hold me in place.

'Yes,' I whispered when I felt him nudging at my entrance.

His chest rumbled with a deep growl when he met my wetness.

'Are you still sore from last night?' he whispered.

I shook my head and he began moving again. I could feel how tight I was around him as he inched his way in. He pressed his face into the crook of my neck and groaned, then pushed himself all the way inside. I gasped at the pressure, and dug my nails into his back.

'Is this okay?' He pulled back to meet my eyes.

I moaned in response and he smiled and began moving again. 'You. Feel. So. Fucking. Good,' he said, peppering my mouth with kisses in between each thrust.

Our breathing and groans grew in volume as we built quickly toward orgasm together.

I didn't know what had possessed him, but he was fucking me hard, pounding me against the wall and I loved this unleashed side of him. 'Logan,' I called, arching my back away from the wall as I came. He wasn't far behind me. A few more deep drives and he uttered something unintelligible and came deep within.

He gazed lovingly into my eyes as he lowered me to my feet and dropped a gentle kiss on my mouth. 'Was that okay?'

'Of course. Why wouldn't it be?'

'I'm sorry if I was too rough with you.' He smoothed my hair away from my face, tucking it behind my ears.

'Well, in case there was any doubt, I liked it very much.'

'Good.' He smiled, looking relieved. 'Come lay down with me.' He tugged my hand towards the bed.

'Just let me clean up first.' I ducked inside the bathroom, chuckling at my image in the mirror. I was still dressed from the waist up, but was naked from the waist down. I wiped myself clean and washed my hands, then returned to my room to find him lying in my bed. He pulled the blankets aside invitingly. 'Come here, beautiful.'

I cuddled in beside him, resting my head on his chest. I liked the way my soft curves fit against the hard length of his body. I listened to the steady rhythm of his heartbeat and wondered again what was going to happen to us when he remembered who he was.

'Logan?' I glanced up and noticed his eyes were closed. I couldn't help myself for being such a girl, but I felt like we needed to talk about our relationship.

'Hm?' He cracked open one eye. 'What sweetheart?'

'What's going to happen when you remember? To us, I mean.'

He stayed quiet for several minutes, but he found my hand and intertwined his fingers between mine. 'You deserve more than what I can give you.'

I wanted to protest. He was kind and loving and smart, but I knew there was some truth to his words too. 'What does that mean?'

'I want to be ready for more, but I'm not yet.'

He was only half a man, how could I expect him to be ready for a relationship? 'Okay,' I said somberly.

'But when I am ready, I know I would be lucky to have you as mine.'

There was nothing else to say, so I closed my eyes and listened to the thumping of his heart and tried not to focus on how badly it might hurt when Logan left.

Logan's nightmares continued each night, but now that he slept in the bed with me, I knew to wake him up and hold him until the trembling went away. Sometimes he would strip me naked and kiss me all over until I was screaming his name, lost in his caresses, other times he'd just lay there and let me hold him, but we didn't make love again.

He also still stayed up late to paint. Painting was the only way he could express the memories trapped in his mind. Several new pictures now decorated my apartment. Most prominently featured were several versions of a white, two-story house, a few of the warehouse he was found in, and a street sign inscribed with the words Mercy Avenue with a park in the distance, but none of them helped us piece his story together any more than the last. It turned out there wasn't even a Mercy Avenue in Chicago, leading us to wonder where that particular memory was from.

I wish I could say the act of painting brought him peace at least, but unfortunately, that wasn't the case. He was tense and on edge until he finished one and then disappointed when it didn't turn out to reveal anything useful. His pain hung thick in the air, filling my apartment with tension. I'd tried to comfort him, and rub his shoulders, but nothing seemed to help. The only time he truly seemed comfortable and at peace was when he was in bed with me at night, holding me and bringing me pleasure.

Chapter Thirteen

As a solution to ease Logan's recent edginess, I suggested we go out to dinner. Logan and I hadn't spent any time together out in public and I didn't like thinking that I was keeping him hidden away in my apartment, like he was someone to be ashamed of.

I talked Logan into trying the Thai restaurant close by, the one with the golden elephant on the sign that I'd wondered about bringing him to. Logan wasn't sure if he liked Thai food, but I explained that introducing him to different sensory experiences could help to provoke a memory.

We were seated at a cozy table in the back where a single votive candle flickered. I couldn't help of thinking of this as a date. I ordered several different dishes for us to try, ginger stir-fry, pad Thai, and chicken satay with curry and peanut sauce. When the food came, Logan tried everything and liked it, but said he wasn't reminded of anything.

At the end of the meal, he insisted on paying, only fueling my belief that this was a date. *Delusional, I know.*

After dinner we strolled down the street, occasionally stopping to look in shop windows. Things were feeling peaceful and domestic between us. Which should have been my first notion that everything was about to change.

We stopped in Grant Park and wandered around the perimeter

as the sun was beginning its descent, turning the sky brilliant hues of pink and orange.

Logan stopped suddenly, his eyes trained across the park. I turned to see what had captured his attention. It was a beat-up silver sedan stopped at the light. A man was standing near the driver's door passing something in through the open window to a guy in the driver's seat. I couldn't tell what had changed hands, but figured it was a drug deal.

My heart rate picked up. Had this captured Logan's attention because of the oddness of the situation, or because it was part of a memory from his past?

With the transaction complete, the man on foot wandered away, stuffing a wad of cash into his pocket.

The guy driving glanced around to ensure he hadn't been spotted, but when he saw Logan, he smiled.

'Hey, man!' The guy waved excitedly. 'Where've you been hiding?' He looked straight at Logan.

Logan's mouth dropped open, and a bewildered expression crossed his face. I could read the question on his face. Somehow he knew this guy?

The light changed to green and the car began to pull away, but the guy stuck his hand out the window and waved. 'Hit me up soon!' he yelled out the window as the car pulled away.

Logan took off, chasing after the car before I had the chance to respond. I jogged behind him, trying to keep up.

The car sped up and was soon lost in the maze of traffic on the busy city street. Logan stopped and bent over, resting his hands on his knees, breathing hard.

'Logan.' I rushed to him. We stood silently watching each other while we caught our breath. There was so much being communicated without us needing to speak a word. Who was he in his past life and what type of people was he involved with?

He released a heavy sigh. 'You shouldn't have seen that.' I tried to make sense of his words, understand what he was guarding me from when he spoke again. 'Go home, Ashlyn. Go back to your life and let me figure out mine.' He pressed a kiss to my forehead and turned away, jogging until he turned a corner and disappeared from sight.

I stood there stunned and unable to move. Logan was gone.

Chapter Fourteen

The next several days dragged on at an agonizing pace. I tossed and turned at night without Logan, worried about where he was sleeping and who would be there for him during his nightmares.

I woke early and spent my days working on campus, trying to keep myself distracted. Even Professor Clancy commented on the dark circles under my eyes, so I'd taken to wearing extra concealer. This was so not like me to be pining over a guy. Except Logan wasn't just any guy. He was a mystery to unravel, a puzzle I desperately wanted to solve, with a heaping dose of sexual chemistry. Not to the mention the deepening feelings I was developing for him despite my better judgment.

On my way to and from campus, I kept thinking I spotted Logan, but of course it was only my mind playing tricks on me. He was gone. Where I didn't know, but I knew he was searching out clues, sparked by that guy in the park.

It scared me to think that he might be targeting drug dealers in search of information. If he was friends with the guy in that car, maybe he was a user too. But his medical records didn't show traces of any drugs in his system. Something just didn't add up.

A knock on my door broke my concentration and I leapt from the chair, my heart galloping. I pulled open the door. It was Liz.

'Oh. It's you.' My face fell.

'Nice to see you too,' Liz muttered, weaving around me to come inside.

Tom immediately came in to greet her and she picked him up. 'So lover boy bailed and left you here with this poor guy?' She kissed the cat on the top of the head.

I didn't answer, but instead let out a deep sigh. The first night Logan had disappeared I'd called Liz. She'd come over to stay with me. I waited up all night for Logan, terrified when he wasn't home by three in the morning that he was going to spend the entire night out, but by dawn, my terror had turned intolerable when I realized he might not come back at all. I sobbed into my pillow as Liz rubbed my back.

I knew she didn't agree with my relationship with Logan in the first place, but I appreciated that she let me fall apart over his sudden disappearance from my life. It was so out of character for me that I think she finally appreciated just how much he meant to me.

I had never expected him to up and leave one day to go discover himself. I'd always imagined he'd only leave if he remembered his former life and wanted to return to it. This way was so much harder to face. He'd rather be alone than be with me. And I couldn't seem to stop my mind from replaying the way he ran from me over and over again.

Liz's pep talks over the last few days were comforting, but bordered on tough love. She didn't want to see me continue to mope around my apartment, and I knew she'd only be so tolerant of me wallowing in my sorrow for a short while longer.

She lifted my stringy hair to her nose as she passed. 'When's the last time you washed this?'

I cringed inwardly. Yesterday? Or had it been the day before?

She released a deep sigh. 'Go take a hot shower. Tom and I will hang out. Then we'll go out and get a drink. Sound okay?'

I nodded and shuffled into the bathroom without complaint. It would be better than sitting in my tiny apartment that still felt full of memories of Logan.

It was too hard to be alone right now, and I needed her company, even if she couldn't understand my pain.

I took my time in the shower, washing my hair, using the jasmine body wash that was a birthday present from Liz and shaving my legs. I felt halfway human again when I finally met her in the living room.

'There's my sexy bitch.' She patted my behind. 'You look better.'

'Thanks,' I mumbled, looking at my shoes. This was the first time I'd put on jeans in days rather than my stretchy yoga pants or leggings, and I was surprised to see that they hung on my hips baggier than before.

I grabbed my purse and we headed for the hallway. When I pulled open the door, I was so stunned at what I saw that it took a moment to register. Logan sat against the far wall, his knees pulled to his chest, his head hanging between his knees. When he heard me gasp, he looked up. He looked awful. Exhaustion and stress had etched purplish hollows under his eyes.

'Logan!' I burst through the entryway and rushed to him, dropping to my knees.

He pulled me to him and kissed my lips, my face, my hair, clutching me desperately. 'Ashlyn.'

'I was so worried.'

'I know.' He kissed my lips again. 'I'm sorry. I had to see if I could figure anything out.'

'And did you?'

His eyes were blank, devoid of hope and I knew the answer before he spoke. He swallowed and tilted his chin up, unable to admit defeat. 'Just that I missed you.'

I hugged him again and he pulled me onto his lap, cradling me.

Liz cleared her throat loudly behind us. 'I guess this means we're not going to get that drink.'

I stood up and offered a hand to Logan. He accepted it and stood. I hated how exhausted he looked, like he hadn't slept at all in the four days he'd been away.

'Sorry, no.' I looked from her to Logan.

She nodded, her lips pressed into a tight line. She began to walk past us, but she stopped directly in front of Logan, and leaned in close. 'It's not okay to use her as your emotional punching bag. Despite how it seems, she's fragile and she has feelings.' She poked him in the chest as she made her point.

Logan looked down, clearly embarrassed at being chastised by her. 'I'm sorry. I know.' Then he turned to me and took my hand, bringing it to his mouth. 'I'm sorry, Ashlyn,' he breathed against the back of my hand.

'It's okay,' I mumbled, mesmerized by the sight of his eyes on mine.

'No, it's not,' Liz scoffed and walked away. 'Call me if you need me,' she hollered from down the hall.

I led him inside the apartment, wanting to interrogate him about where he had been, what he had discovered, but I kept my mouth shut, sensing that he needed some space. He headed into the shower, while I heated up a can of soup.

I laid a set of fresh clothes for him on the bed and waited anxiously for him to get out of the shower. In my head I planned out how to initiate the talk I knew we needed to have. I lit some candles around the apartment, hoping to set a calming mood. Logan needed help. As the professional, levelheaded one in this relationship, it was time that I pointed that out to him.

He emerged from the shower clean-shaven and smelling fresh. He joined me on the couch and I offered him a mugful of soup. He accepted it gratefully and sipped the warm broth eagerly from the edge of the mug. When he had finished the soup, he set the mug on the coffee table and pulled me into his lap.

I settled onto his lap, curling against his frame while he wrapped his arms around me. My courage over the discussion we needed to have faded just slightly. It felt so good to have him back I didn't want to disturb this reverie.

'I can feel your ribs,' he murmured against my neck.

'I didn't do so well when you left,' I admitted.

He swore under his breath. 'I left to make things easier on you. I didn't like thinking I was weighing you down, complicating your life.'

'You weren't. I wanted you here.'

He nodded carefully. 'I know that now. I'm sorry I took off like that.'

'Where did you go?'

He swallowed the lump in his throat and stayed quiet. 'Everywhere. I roamed the streets, talked to some dealers. I asked around, but I couldn't turn up any leads.'

I sat up straighter, summoning my courage. 'Logan, I care about you, and I can't watch you do this to yourself. Having amnesia is not your fault. And no matter who you were before, I can tell that you have a good heart.'

He closed his eyes at my words, struggling to keep quiet.

'I want you to stay here with me, but I think you need to get some professional help. Talk to someone. Maybe get some medication. I know you wanted to solve all this on your own, but...'

He lifted me from his lap and stood, leaving me sitting alone on the sofa. He began pacing the living room. 'I don't want some fucking doctor prying into shit, asking me questions I can't answer, or asking me about feelings I can't explain.' He stood with his back to me, looking out the window to the street below. 'I need to do this my way, Ashlyn. I won't take off again if that's what you're worried about.'

'No.' The anger and vehemence in my voice surprised us both. Logan spun around to face me. 'That's not going to work. I want you here, and I want to be in your life. But this isn't living.' I struggled to find the right words. 'You need to get help. And unless you agree to that, I don't think you should be here.'

I stood and fled to my bedroom before he could see the tears filling my eyes. Even if this pushed him away, I knew I needed to stand my ground. We couldn't go on living the way we had. Logan needed help.

A few minutes later, my bedroom door opened and Logan peeked inside. I was pacing, waiting to see what he'd do. He came in and closed the door behind him, and walked closer to me.

'Okay.'

'Okay?' I asked.

'I'll see whatever doctors you think I should, talk to shrinks, do hypnosis, whatever you think will help. I just want to stay with you. You're all I have, Ashlyn.'

I should have felt happy and relieved that he was going to seek help, but something nagged at me. I was all he had in this world. Did he actually have real feelings for me? Or was I just his only source of food and shelter?

I continued staring at him impassively. 'I need more than that,' I found myself saying. It nearly crushed me when he left and now that he was back, I couldn't put off this conversation any longer.

He waited for me to continue, but when I remained quiet he took my hand and led me over to the bed. 'Sit down. Tell me.'

'When you left, I did a lot of thinking. About you, and about us. I need to know why you're here. Why you missed me. Was it because I'm the only person you know in Chicago, because I can offer you a place to sleep at night?' Maybe Liz's ranting had started to seep into my brain. Her critical judgments of Logan seemed a little more justified now. If he could just leave so easily, was he using me?

He curled his hands into fists. 'You don't get it. I tried to leave to protect you. A guy like me will never fit into your life.'

'Logan,' I sighed. Conversations with him sometimes exhausted me and left me more confused than before.

'You've done far more than I deserve. I don't understand what it is you could possibly see in me. I have nothing to offer a woman like you. You're beautiful, brilliant, and being with you--hurting you--scares the shit out of me.'

'But,' I supplied for him, at his pained expression.

'But despite all of that, I'm falling for you. You're delicate, and smart, and a damn terrible housekeeper.' He chuckled, running his thumb across my bottom lip. 'I want to protect you and make you happy.'

I smiled like an idiot, gazing up into his eyes. Maybe it was foolish of me, but I was in no way ready to remove Logan from my life.

He leaned in and softly kissed my lips. 'Have you eaten dinner?'

I shook my head.

'Let's go feed you. You're getting too thin.'

He led me from my room, and sat me down on a stool in the kitchen so I could watch him cook. When dinner was ready, he made me finish every bite of the spaghetti until I was full.

After dinner, he tucked me against his side on the couch while he looked up local psychiatrists and doctors online who specialized in amnesia. Dr. Andrews' name kept appearing in the searches, until finally Logan relented and we clicked the link to request an appointment.

As I lay in bed that night while Logan went to paint, I tried to quiet my fears about his past and about our future, and just enjoy the small comforts of having him here while I could, even if it wouldn't last.

Chapter Fifteen

I was a jittery mess as we waited in the exam room for Dr. Andrews. Logan sat in the side chair, leaving me to climb onto the paper-covered exam table, like somehow his choice of seating meant he wasn't the patient. I sat at the end of the table, the paper crinkling underneath me as I swung my ankles restlessly back and forth.

'Stop fidgeting. Why are you so nervous?' Logan asked.

I wrapped my arms around myself. It was just too damn quiet in this room and I flinched at the footsteps I could hear in the hall.

Dr. Andrews had suspected that Logan and I were growing close already back when he was a patient in the hospital, so showing up with him today would confirm that my relationship with Logan went well beyond a professional one. I might as well be wearing a flashing neon sign declaring me a wanton hussy.

'If you didn't want the doctor to see you with me, you didn't have to come,' he said harshly.

'No. I want to be here.' I did. We had talked about this last night once Logan had washed the paint from his hands and climbed into bed. We weren't going to let the circumstances surrounding the way we met stop us from being together. It was very freeing. There would be no more hiding, no more tiptoeing around the conversation. Logan and I were together, plain and simple. We cared for each other and were doing what felt right.

That didn't stop my stomach from sinking the second door swung open. Dr. Andrews strode into the room, casting a cautionary glance in my direction before turning his attention to Logan.

Dr. Andrews sat down, situated a pair of tiny spectacles on the end of his nose and opened the file containing a mass of papers across his knees. After asking Logan a few basic questions, Dr. Andrews turned to me. 'Why don't you step outside?'

'She's staying,' Logan said, his tone ringing with finality.

Dr. Andrews narrowed his eyes, clearly not liking his directions being ignored. He removed his glasses and tucked them into his coat pocket. I could tell he was dying to ask what type of relationship we had, but having no medical reason for that information, it remained unspoken.

He concluded that the effects of Logan's concussion and previous injuries were gone, and he was healthy and well, aside from not remembering the past twenty-some years of his life.

'I'm glad you came back in. I'd like to perform periodic neurological evaluations to check on your progress and to see if you are recovering any old memories or forming new ones.'

Logan nodded his consent.

'Are you able to recall details and recent memories? Any trouble remembering what you did yesterday?' Dr. Andrews asked.

'I remember everything since the day I woke up in the hospital. But still nothing from before.'

After finishing up with a few more questions, and offering suggestions on vitamin supplements, Dr. Andrews turned to me. 'He'll provide a very interesting piece for your amnesia publication.'

I ignored his implied message--that I was using Logan to get ahead in my research. 'Let's go home, Logan.'

Logan nodded and took my arm, helping me down from the exam table.

We were silent on the train ride home since there wasn't much to talk about after his appointment. I'd been so set on Logan getting help, but I'd been grasping at straws. Still, it meant a lot to me that he'd agreed to go.

Logan got off at the stop near my apartment. At the next stop, I set off on foot to meet Liz for coffee. I hadn't spoken to her since Logan had returned and I wasn't even sure we were still on for our standing coffee date, but when I'd sent her a text asking if she wanted to meet, she'd replied enthusiastically with, *Of course!!*

When I got to the coffee shop, Liz hadn't yet arrived. The bells on the door chimed and Liz came strolling in, dressed in workout clothes. She'd just gotten done with her run by the looks of it. She plopped herself down into the chair across from me.

'Oh, thank God.' She reached for the large iced Americano I'd ordered for her and began sucking it down.

Liz drank coffee like most people drank water. I sipped my warm latte and watched her, wondering if we were going to talk about the elephant in the room.

After a few more healthy gulps, and with her breathing now returning to normal, Liz lowered her drink to the table. 'Listen, I don't want you thinking I hate him, because that's not the case. I'm just worried about you.'

I appreciated how she never beat around the bush. 'I'm worried too. I've been guarding my heart for the past twenty years. I grew up without the usual affection and love most families have. You know me. I hardly date. I wasn't looking for anything. And I certainly never intended to fall for a test subject.'

She scoffed, cracking a smile. 'I get it. Your mom was gone and your dad put food on the table, but that was it. Logan's different, and you care about him.'

'Very much,' I admitted.

'So what happens when he takes off again?'

I noted she said *when* and not *if*, but I let it go. 'You'll be there for me.'

She nodded once. 'Fair enough.'

We sipped our coffee in silence for a few minutes more, until I saw a flash of an idea in her eyes. 'Now that he's your boyfriend, we should all go out, introduce him around to the gang. I'll round up some friends.'

'Hm. I don't know if that's a good idea, Liz.'

'We'll go out and grab a drink, something casual, low key. It'll be fun.'

'Sure. I guess so,' I mumbled, knowing I'd never be able to dissuade Liz once she was set on an idea.

Chapter Sixteen

Logan dressed in the new gray button-down shirt I'd bought for him, and rolled the sleeves up to his elbows. 'How will you explain me to your friends?'

I waved my hand. 'Don't worry about it. They'll be cool with it.' The truth was, I had no idea how to introduce him to my friends. *The amnesia patient I was sleeping with? Boyfriend? Friend? Roommate?* I took another healthy swig of my wine. It was a little depressing to think that the one man I'd opened myself up to had mental issues and a likely criminal record. *Nice, Ashlyn.* It wasn't exactly a winning endorsement of my track record with guys. Regardless, I wanted to have fun tonight, to loosen him up and show him that we fit in each other's lives.

I'd told Logan it was a night out to celebrate that my thesis proposal had been accepted, and it was, but more than that, it would be our coming out in public as a couple.

I pulled at my navy skirt, persuading it to inch closer towards my knees. Paired with a fitted cream top, I looked every bit the professional doctorate student I was, but my brown knee-high boots lent a bit of edge to the look.

Logan ran his hands down my back, and stopped at my backside, appreciatively giving me a generous squeeze. 'Seeing you in these boots and short skirt makes me want to bend you over and fuck you right here,' he whispered near my ear. A thrill skittered down my spine.

'As tempting as that sounds,' I pressed a kiss to his lips, 'you'll have to hold that thought. Liz has arranged this whole thing, and I don't want to keep everyone waiting for us.'

He met my eyes. 'And if you showed up with bedroom hair and flushed pink skin, they would know I just fucked you. Because I don't plan on holding back tonight.'

I groaned. 'Do we have to go?'

He chuckled at me. 'Come on. We'll make our appearance. Then you're mine. And if you keep me out too long, I'm not above fucking you at the table in front of your friends.'

I drained the rest of my wine and grabbed his hand. 'Come on. Let's go.' *Let's get this over with,* I added silently in my head.

We reached the bar, which was more of a swanky lounge, and were directed to a table in the back by an overeager hostess who displayed an unhealthy interest in Logan. I shot her an evil look. *Bitch, please. He's with me.*

Liz leaped up from the table when she spotted us. She pulled me in for a hug, and greeted Logan more coolly, with a wave and a nod of her head. We sat in the center of the table, me in between Liz and Logan, and friends from our program, a sweet Asian girl named Kim, and Porter, who had asked me out several times at the beginning of the year.

I'd mentioned to Logan on the walk over that I wanted a glass of champagne tonight, and when the waitress came by for our order, he ordered a bottle of champagne for the table and a gin and tonic for himself. I patted his knee under the table. 'Thank you.'

He slung his arm around my chair, leaning back causally. Kim was too polite to grill him with questions, but the appraising look on Porter's face told me that he'd have no such qualms regarding this mysterious man I'd brought with me.

When our drinks arrived, Logan poured the glasses of champagne and Liz finished her story about the lovesick undergrad who was still following her around after their date several weeks ago.

Porter kept his eyes trained on Logan, and leaned forward on his elbows. 'So how'd you two meet?'

I flashed Logan a panicked look, but his face was calm. 'I've got this one, babe,' he said with a wink. 'We met at Northwestern Memorial as part of a project Ashlyn was working on.'

I let out a little sigh of relief. It was entirely true, but Logan had worded it so that Porter and Kim would assume he was a resident, or employee of the hospital.

'Interesting.' Porter nodded.

'What are you studying?' Logan asked, subtly directing the conversation away from himself.

I grinned at his cleverness. Getting Porter to talk about himself was genius. Porter couldn't resist--it was his favorite topic--and one of the main reasons I'd turned him down. He was self-absorbed. But more than that, I just wasn't attracted to him. He wasn't bad looking, but he was only a few inches taller than me, and scrawny, lacking in the testosterone and overt maleness I was attracted to. Glancing between him and Logan--there was no comparison. Logan could pass for a male model. Even more than that, it was his confidence that I found incredibly sexy. He casually leaned back, draping his arm across my chair as he listened to Porter's response.

'What do you do at the hospital?' Porter asked.

'I was working with Dr. Andrews. But right now I'm contracted to paint a mural at a school for underprivileged youth.'

'Aw,' Liz and Kim chimed in unison.

Porter narrowed his eyes at Logan. *Why was he acting so strange?*

'So, Logan, did you grow up around here?' *Sheesh, what was with Porter's intense line of questioning?*

Logan took a sip of his drink. 'Here and there.' He looked cool and collected, but my stomach was doing the cha-cha on crack. He reached under the table and squeezed my knee in reassurance.

I took another sip of champagne, trying to relax, and listened to Liz pump Kim for information on which guys in our program she thought were cute. Kim's expression was like a deer in a car's headlights. Poor dear, but I couldn't intervene. If the focus was on Kim's love life, at least for the time being it meant Liz would stay out of mine.

Not gathering anything of interest, Liz stood abruptly. 'Oh! I love this song. Let's go dance.' She pulled Kim and me from our seats. 'Girls dance!'

I turned to Logan, not wanting to leave him alone with Porter. 'Come dance with me.'

'I don't dance, sweetheart.' He smirked.

Porter drained his glass of beer. 'I'll dance with you.'

I frowned as Porter stood to follow me and I trailed behind Liz and Kim to the dance floor. I hadn't wanted to leave Logan alone, but maybe he'd appreciate a minute to himself. This was a lot to take in since we'd spent the last several weeks practically secluded in my apartment. I followed the group to the center of the dance floor and began swaying in time with the music.

I wasn't much for dancing, but Liz insisted on it every time we went out, so I knew it was easier to give in and sway with her on the dance floor, rather than have her fight me until I gave in. And I never liked making others unhappy, even if it meant doing something I didn't really want to do. Watching Liz twirl and shimmy with a big smile on her face, I supposed it was worth it.

I glanced over at Logan. He had slouched comfortably in his chair with his drink raised to his lips, looking smug as he watched me.

I was never the center of attention when dancing next to Liz, but Logan kept his eyes trained to my body. I recalled his promise when we got home and smiled at him.

I swayed under his promising gaze, his attention giving me a dose of confidence. I closed my eyes and let the music guide me, rocking my hips in time with the beat. I felt a pair of firm hands grasp me around the waist, and I smiled, opening my eyes, hoping to find that Logan had joined me. Disappointingly, I discovered it was Porter. My smile instantly fell.

'Don't stop now. That was damn sexy,' he said over the music.

I stepped away from his roaming hands. 'Porter,' I warned.

Logan stepped in between Porter and me. 'How about you keep your hands to yourself?' he said, his gaze lowering to Porter's.

Porter held up his hands in surrender. 'Relax. You said you didn't want to dance. I was just having fun with her.'

Logan held Porter's gaze for a few seconds longer. Just as suddenly as he'd come to my rescue, he snaked his arms around my middle and swept me away to a more private corner of the dance floor.

He pressed his forehead to mine, his breath whispering over my mouth. 'I didn't like seeing his hands on you.'

I smiled in return. 'I had the situation handled.'

'I know,' he quickly added, not wanting to insult me.

Logan and I continued dancing close together, gently swaying to the beat of our own music. I dared a glance back at Liz and Kim who had found a group of guys to dance with. Porter sat at the table, drinking his beer and pouting. *Real mature.*

I pushed Porter's odd behavior from my mind and focused on Logan who was pressed up against me in the warm, dark club.

I loved how being out with Logan made me feel. Carefree. Alive. Daring. Everything I wasn't during my day-to-day life. He was attentive and focused solely on me, though I saw several girls admiring him.

His body close to mine did delicious things to me. I turned around so my backside was pressed against his crotch. He gripped my hips while I slowly moved my body, dancing close against him.

For the briefest of moments I worried that I looked like an idiot, but then I felt his growing erection straining against his jeans. It was a very powerful feeling knowing I was turning him on in public. I nearly giggled at the thought. Then Logan leaned down close to my ear and I could feel his breath hitch.

'Damn it, Ashlyn. I'm not above taking you in the bathroom to fuck you. Now behave.' He swatted my ass.

I whimpered at the shock of it and turned around to face him, my mouth still agape.

'Are you going to behave?' he whispered, just loud enough to be heard above the music.

I found myself nodding. 'If you take me home soon.'

His eyes gleamed with his arousal. 'Let's go.' He tugged my hand, guiding me off the dance floor.

'We need to say goodbye.' I pulled him in the direction of the table and my friends.

He groaned, but followed behind me dutifully. I glanced down at his jeans to see if the evidence of his arousal was still visible. He caught me looking and chuckled. 'I'm presentable. For now.'

When we went back to the table to say goodbye, I hugged the girls while Logan gave Porter an icy handshake.

Logan's mouth was on mine before we were even inside the apartment. He pulled me close in a full body embrace and kicked the door closed behind us.

His initial reluctance to share himself with me now seemed like a lifetime ago as he eagerly kissed and nipped at my lips. We bumped into each other and knocked against the furniture as we clumsily made our way into the dining room without breaking the kiss. It was a mutually unspoken agreement that the ten steps to the bedroom was too far to go.

Logan walked me backwards until I bumped into the dining room table. 'You. Are. Mine.'

I wondered if Porter's attention tonight had anything to do with his declaration, but he was clearly on edge tonight. 'Of course, Logan. Yours. Only yours.'

He kissed me again, and I fumbled to grip the edges of the table as my legs suddenly became unstable. My hand brushed against one of his paintings and I looked down to ensure I hadn't messed up any wet paint. The image of the exotic woman was staring back up at me. The one and only person he ever painted was her, and there were now half a dozen of them. I pulled away from his kisses and frowned down at the portrait. 'Logan, move your painting.'

'It's fine,' he murmured, leaning in to kiss me again.

I pushed him away far enough to give myself some breathing room. 'I can't do this with *her* watching.'

He drew his eyebrows together, visibly confused. 'Her?' He looked down at the offending painting, realizing the mysterious woman and his history with her had upset me.

He grabbed the painting, carried it across the room and stuffed it unceremoniously in the closet before shutting the door. Then he came back to me, and took my face in his hands, looking me straight in the eyes. 'I don't want that to upset you. I don't even know who she is. It's you and me, okay?'

For now, my inner pessimist pointed out, intent to get in the last word.

He smoothed his thumbs across my cheeks. 'Okay, baby?'

I nodded, unable to keep my lower lip from jutting out.

'I didn't know she upset you,' he murmured, tucking my hair behind my ears.

I released a deep sigh. 'Logan, how could she not? She's probably your girlfriend.'

'She's someone I remember nothing about--how much could she have possibly meant to me?'

I didn't point out that he remembered every detail of her physical appearance--enough to have half a dozen portraits of her all identical in their resemblance. Instead I tried a different tactic. 'Each time you've seen another man show any interest in me--like my date with Jason and then tonight with Porter, you've gone all caveman on me and practically dragged me to your side to fuck me.' I flinched at the harshness in my words.

Logan cocked his head studying me, examining if what I said was accurate.

'Can you imagine how much worse that would feel if I had reciprocated and I was the one who was interested in them? You painting her again and again, yeah, it hurts, Logan.'

'I'm sorry. I thought...you always encouraged me to try and remember, to explore whatever memories I could. Painting is the only way I can do that. She could be my sister for all I know.'

I bit my lip to avoiding reminding him of the painting of her in a bed wearing only a sheet. That painting now resided in the farthest back corner of my storage closet. *Sister, my ass.*

'First thing tomorrow, I'll get rid of all those paintings. She doesn't matter to me. Listen to me, Ashlyn.' He gripped my hands, lacing his fingers between mine. 'You are with me now. You're all I want.'

A slow grin spread across my face. I should have been offended hearing him claim me as his--I was no one's property--but instead it touched me. He was facing his fears about opening up and getting close to someone. I didn't know exactly when he decided I was worth the risk, but it thrilled me just the same. 'Yes, Logan. You're all I want, too.'

'There's only you,' he whispered, meeting my gaze with his expressive hazel eyes.

113

My heart pounded in my chest, and I had the sudden feeling like we'd crossed some barrier together. He lifted me by the hips and sat me on the edge of the dining room table, admiring my dangling legs and boots with a sexy grin. He trailed a single fingertip across my bare knee, up my thigh and just under the edge of my skirt.

'And just to clarify my caveman behavior, that guy Jason was a tool. And between Porter's Q and A session with me and then treating you like you were a novelty to entertain him… If I hadn't stepped away when I did, I would have decked him.'

'Shut up and kiss me already.'

He lowered his mouth and brushed his lips across mine, taking his time, letting my anticipation build. I parted my lips, ready for more. His tongue swept across my bottom lip, tasting, teasing.

Thinking I could speed things up and break through his control, I grabbed onto his belt loops and hauled him closer, fumbling with his belt buckle. He chuckled against my mouth. 'Impatient much?'

His belt must have been booby-trapped or childproof or something, but the damn buckle wouldn't open. Without taking his lips from mine, his hands took pity on and joined the mission, easily releasing the clasp. I worked my hands inside the front of his trousers to find he was already hard. He let out a soft grunt when my fingers encased him, stroking gently. With each stroke I felt his hips respond, moving closer toward me. He was so incredibly sexy.

After a few minutes more of kissing and fondling, he pulled away, passion blazing in his eyes. He reached under my skirt and tugged my panties down. I lifted my bottom from the table to aid his task. He took his time, bending down to remove them from over my boots, then dropping them to the floor. When he stood again with his impressive erection jutting out in front of him, I released a soft whimper.

'Shh. Come here.' He dragged my hips closer to him, which pushed the skirt up as I scooted to the edge of the table. He teasingly rubbed me, his fingers sliding easily over my wet folds. He pushed my thighs further apart and situated himself in front of me. He continued stroking my sensitive bud until I was writhing against his chest, balling his shirt into my fists. 'Logan…I'm going to…'

He pressed his lips to mine. 'I know. Come for me, baby.' He slid one finger inside me as he continued to massage my clit. The sensations were heavenly. 'God, I want to fuck you,' he breathed into my neck. His dirty whispers brought me right over the edge. I planted my hands behind me on the table, needing the support as I arched my hips forward. An intense eruption of pleasure burst from my core.

Logan wasted no time pushing his thick cock against my entrance. I was still trembling form the aftershocks of my orgasm when I felt him slide inside me. I was slick and wet, but still, each inch of him stretched me to capacity and I groaned out his name.

He leaned back to admire where our bodies were joined, thrusting into me slowly while holding my knees apart. I bit my lip to keep from screaming. 'Logan.'

'Fuck, you're tight, baby.'

'Does it hurt you?' I asked.

His lips curved into a sexy smirk. 'It's the best fucking feeling in the world.' He leaned in close to kiss my lips. I grasped onto his shoulders, needing to grip him for support. He brought his hands to my ass, hauling me even closer and driving into me at the same time. 'Ashlyn,' he whispered.

Logan pumped into me hard, driving deeper than ever before. His breathing was heavy and delicious near my ear, his gasps brief and sharp as he came. I tingled all over at the intimacy of the act, despite both of us still being fully clothed.

Logan pulled out of me, and kissed my forehead. 'You are amazing.' I smiled at his compliment. I had done little more than perch on the edge of the table and take all the pleasure he could give me. But that seemed to please him.

He tucked himself back inside his pants while I contemplated the most ladylike way to get down from the table, and wondered if my legs would even support my weight right now.

Luckily, before I had to fully plan my strategy, Logan lifted me from the table and carried me into my bedroom, not setting me down until I was on the bed.

'Thanks for the lift, but I still have to change and get cleaned up.'

He kissed me again and left me to get changed. I wondered if he planned to paint tonight, but by the time I had used the bathroom and put on my tank top and sleeping shorts, he'd returned, setting a glass of water on my night table.

'Drink this. I don't want you to feel hungover in the morning.'

'Thanks.' I pressed the glass to my lips. I'd only had two glasses of champagne, but still I liked the little things he thought to do for me.

We pulled back the blankets and both slipped in, migrating to the center of the bed to be near each other.

Chapter Seventeen

I woke up the next morning to my phone vibrating nosily against my nightstand. I fumbled for it, knocking the alarm clock off the edge, sending it clattering to the floor. It was Porter. I frowned at the caller ID, trying to understand why Porter would be calling me early on a Saturday morning.

He hadn't contacted me in months. There was a time that I regretted giving him my number. While his occasional calls started out innocently enough, like calling to get something he missed in class, they eventually progressed to late night ramblings, asking me if I was up for hanging out. I'd stopped answering my phone until he got the picture. Even so, he had never called me so early before.

'Hello?' I rasped, trying not to wake Logan.

'Um, hey Ash, I didn't wake you up, did I?'

'No.' I didn't know why my automatic response to that question was always no, like I was embarrassed to be found sleeping, it was only eight in the morning after all. I surveyed the bed next to me, noting Logan was already up. I flung the covers from my legs and stretched. 'What's up?'

'Well, this is going to sound strange, but I wanted to talk to you about Logan.'

Oh sheesh, give it rest, I thought. *I am not interested in you, Porter.* 'What about?'

'Actually, I was hoping you'd meet me for coffee this morning so I could explain.'

'Porter, I thought I'd made it clear, I'm not interested.'

'That's not what this is about. I just…may have some information on Logan you should hear.'

My stomach dropped. 'Ah. Yeah, sure. The Imperial Room okay?'

'Sure. Twenty minutes?' he asked.

'See you there.'

I hung up the phone and got changed. After brushing my teeth, I found Logan in the living room putting on his shoes. 'Morning. Are you headed out?' I asked.

'Yeah.' He kept his eyes down and pulled on his other shoe.

Oh. I wondered where he was going.

'There's just something I need to take care of this morning,' he said, answering my unspoken question. 'I'll be back soon.' He kissed me on the cheek and headed out the door.

I stood there for a few extra minutes, thrown off that I hadn't even had to make up an excuse about going out.

Moments later, I was out the door and headed down the street to the coffee shop. Porter was already waiting inside at a table by the front window. There was a steaming mug of coffee set in front of him and a tall mug with a latte at the spot across from him. He remembered my coffee order; it was both thoughtful, and weird.

'This for me?' I asked as I approached the table and pulled out a chair.

Porter nodded and began to stand, but I motioned for him to stay seated.

I took a cautious sip of the latte, but when I discovered it wasn't too hot, took a long drink. *Mmm.* The bitter espresso and frothy steamed milk were a brilliant combination and just what I needed to ease my nerves over whatever it was that Porter had to say.

'So…' I began.

'So.' He smiled, playing coy. 'Where to begin…' He strummed his fingers on the edge of the table.

'Porter. Just tell me what you know.' I braced myself by wrapping my hands around the warmth of the mug.

He swallowed. 'Okay, first off I know how you really met Logan. At the end of the night, Liz was a little drunk, and she let it slip that Logan has amnesia.'

Oh shit. Liz would be getting a lesson in Secret Keeping 101. 'And…' I prompted.

'And he looked familiar to me. That's why I was asking all those questions earlier in the night. But I figured he just had a look-alike out there, or I didn't remember clearly.'

My heart thumped in my chest, my palms dampening more from nervousness than from the temperature of the mug. 'Remember what?'

'I think he used to date my roommate's good friend.'

It was the strangest sensation of wanting to know yet not wanting to hear what Porter would say next. 'Your roommate Shelby?' Porter's roommate was a nice, hippie-type girl I'd met once before when Liz and I had picked Porter up for a study session. I remembered Shelby sitting cross-legged on the floor, long hair hanging in her face while she knitted something out of hemp.

'Yeah, I remember him coming around once or twice a while ago. He dated one of her friends, named, um…Logan.'

Holy fuck!

I guess that explained the tattoo. I swallowed a thick lump in my throat. The latte felt like it was burning away the lining in my esophagus.

'Ash? Are you okay? You're looking a little pale.'

'I'm fine. Just, please continue.'

He sighed, and ran his hands through his hair. 'I wasn't sure it was the same guy. His hair's shorter for one. But when he acted all possessive with you, I was pretty damn positive it was him. I remember Shelby saying he had a jealous streak and did the same thing with Logan, like he needed to mark his territory.'

Oh.

'So who is he?'

Porter shook his head. 'I can't remember his name. I only met him once.'

'Why are you telling me this? What happened to him and Logan? Do you think Shelby knows anything?' My heart pounded faster, like I was on some secret mission and was about to be discovered at any moment.

'Shelby will know all the details, I'm sure. But I didn't know if you'd want me to include her. I didn't want this getting out and compromising your research, but I trust Shelby. She'll be discreet.'

'Yes, I need to talk to her. I have to know.'

He nodded. 'The only thing is…'

'What?'

'Shelby's out of town for a few days. Do you have a picture of him on your phone or something, so we can at least confirm it's him?'

I was about to answer no when I suddenly remembered the stupid shot I'd snapped of him with Tom when he'd first brought him home. I dug through my bag and produced my phone. It took me three tries to get the passcode right and then several fumbling attempts to pull up my photo album since my hands were shaking so badly.

It was a close up shot and you could clearly see Logan's face in the frame as he smiled at the camera. I turned it to show Porter.

'Good, that will work. I wanted to show his picture to Shelby to make sure it was him before I got you all worked up over nothing.'

I nodded, it seemed like a good idea. Porter typed her email into my phone and I sent the photo. Tapping my finger against the send key felt like a direct hit to my relationship with Logan. I'd always told him I'd trusted him. But now, facing the truth, I needed some time to process it alone and examine what it would mean for us.

'Just be careful, okay?' Porter said, his hand reaching across the table to squeeze mine.

'I will. Do you know anything else, about him and Logan, I mean?'

He frowned. 'I only caught bits and pieces secondhand through Shelby. I know it ended badly and that Logan was in the hospital after they broke up.'

I pushed the coffee away from me as my stomach twisted violently.

Porter gave my hand another squeeze. 'It's going to be okay. Let's talk later. Maybe I'll have heard back from Shelby,' Porter suggested.

'Don't call,' I blurted suddenly. 'Logan lives with me. Just text or email.'

He shook his head. 'Geez, Ashlyn. You don't even know this guy.'

'I know, all right? Don't rub it in.' I didn't need his disapproval too; I already got plenty of that from Liz.

'Fine. Let's just figure this out together, okay?'

I nodded. 'Thanks for your help.' Having Porter's help in this eased my anxiety just a bit. I left my coffee mug in the bussing tray near the door, and strode out into the cool fall air. Movement caught the corner of my eye and I glanced up just in time to see Logan crossing the street, headed in the opposite direction. Had he been watching me with Porter? A chill skittered up my spine, and I wrapped my cardigan tighter around myself, picking up my pace towards home.

Chapter Eighteen

Neither Logan nor I spoke about spotting each other outside the coffee shop. I started to believe maybe he hadn't seen me, but one morning a few days later when I got ready to leave, telling him I was having coffee with friends, he turned to me and said, 'Tell Porter I say hello.'

My stomach clenched with nerves. He had seen me, but neither of us was willing to admit what we had been up to that morning. It went both ways. It felt deceptive going about things this way, but I needed answers. I wanted to be with this man, and I desperately needed him to want to be with me. We needed to know the truth before we could truly have a relationship that consisted of more than just sharing a bed.

I'd merely nodded weakly at him and slipped out the door, scurrying to the coffee shop as though demons were on my tail. When I got inside, Porter and Shelby hadn't yet arrived, so I got in line to order. I purchased a tea hoping it would help calm me, but I was too nervous to drink it and it sat growing cold on the table.

Finally, the bells on the door chimed and I glanced up to see Porter and Shelby entering. Shelby was just like I remembered her, with long tangled tresses and a kind, but unkempt look about her. I stood up and shook both their hands, not knowing what else to do with myself. I was a nervous wreck.

Porter hadn't told me much, just that Shelby had recognized the picture and wanted to meet with me, which made whatever this was seem all the more ominous.

'So, do you know the guy in the picture?' I asked her, unable to wait for even a nanosecond of silence.

'Yeah. That's Aiden.'

'Aiden,' I repeated. The name felt foreign on my tongue.

'Yep, Aiden York, the youngest Art History professor ever to work at Northwestern.'

Art. History. The pieces mentally clicked into place. 'What else do you know about him?'

Shelby bit her lip. 'Porter, will you go and order us some coffee?'

He nodded and stood from the table.

Shelby swallowed and continued. 'I'm sure there are two sides to every story.' She twisted her hands on the table. 'Logan's relationship with him was passionate, but rocky. They met down in Memphis where Aiden was contracted to paint a mural for a bar one summer a couple of years ago. Logan's an artist too and was there for a summer seminar.'

My stomach was a tense knot of nerves, and I tucked my hands into my lap, waiting for her to continue.

'So where's Logan now? Were… are they still together?' If I had the chance to help Logan--Aiden, I corrected myself--to get his identity back, I would. Even if the truth would mean the end of my relationship with him.

Shelby sighed. 'Things ended badly between them, and I'm not sure how much Logan would want me to tell you. I'll have to check first.'

I couldn't bring myself to ask anything further. I wasn't ready to have my entire world come crashing down all at once.

I scrawled my phone number, email address and postal address down on the back of an old receipt for Shelby. 'Please. Let me know whatever you can.'

She nodded. 'I will.'

The urge to search the web on my phone for Aiden York pulled at me. Even though I was investigating him behind his back, that was where I drew the line. It nearly killed me not to start up the web browser on the walk home. I stuffed my earbuds in instead and cranked up the music to an ungodly level to avoid even thinking.

I didn't go home right away. I couldn't face Logan, or Aiden or whoever the hell he was. So many thoughts swirled in my mind. What exactly had happened between him and Logan? Did their relationship mean that he was gay and he was just…confused with me? How had an art history Professor ended up that in that dingy warehouse that day? Even with this new information, there were still too many unanswered questions.

I sat on the train and listened to my music, blankly staring out the window as the thoughts swirled in my mind. I kept my earbuds firmly in place to discourage any chatty strangers.

Later that afternoon, I found myself wandering down Lakeshore drive, but when the passing couples holding hands became too much, I fled down a side street. I indulged myself in a chocolate ice cream cone from a street vendor after realizing I hadn't eaten all day. Then to avoid going home just yet, ventured into a cute boutique and bought myself a few new tops and a pair of jeans.

When I knew I couldn't avoid the situation with Logan/Aiden any longer, I finally got the train headed towards home.

I let myself inside and tossed my bag of clothes on the floor. 'Logan?' I called out in the seemingly empty apartment.

'In the kitchen,' he called.

His voice instantly calmed me. What was I so afraid of? We were perfect together. I held on to the tiniest bit of hope that everything would work out. I leaned against the doorframe to the kitchen, watching as he laid lightly floured chicken breasts into a skillet simmering with butter.

He looked up and smiled. 'I found a recipe for chicken marsala online today.' He tossed in a handful of sliced mushrooms and splashed the pan with a gush of Marsala wine.

'It smells awesome.' The garlicky aroma coming from my kitchen was mouthwatering.

He washed and dried his hands at the sink. 'Come here, baby.' I obeyed, walking silently towards him.

He pulled me into his arms and kissed my mouth. 'Why'd you leave all day?' he murmured.

'Sorry. I just needed to get out.'

He pulled back and studied me with a confused expression. He had just opened his mouth to speak when a light knocking on the door caught our attention.

'Who could be here?' I wondered, as I moved away from him to answer.

The knocking continued until I reached the door and pulled it open.

A breathtakingly beautiful woman stood before me, looking frazzled. She was thin and petite with dark hair and glowing olive skin. I got a nagging feeling, and it took me only a second to make the connection--she was the woman from the paintings.

I stood there, mouth open, taking her in. A dozen questions formed in my head, not the least of which was, what was she doing here?

'I'm…um, looking for Aiden.' She rose onto her toes to peek around me into the apartment.

'Who are you?' I didn't mean the bitchy tone in my voice, it just inserted itself into the question.

'I'm Logan.' She smiled a dazzling megawatt smile that made my knees weak and my stomach turn queasy. Holy shit! *This* was Logan?

Logan/Aiden must have heard her voice from the other room, because when I turned around, he was standing in the doorway with a dishtowel draped over one shoulder and his face a mix of emotions.

'Aiden,' her voice broke and she rushed to him, jumping into his arms, knocking them both to the floor with a thud. She plastered her body to his, attacking his mouth and face with kisses. He seemed stunned, but didn't push her away.

It was sickening to watch, but like a bad car accident, I couldn't look away.

After several seconds of her mauling him on the floor, he stood and helped her to her feet. Her cheeks were flushed pink and her smile could not be dampened. She clung to his side like a needy puppy.

I hadn't realized it, but tears had welled in my eyes and were threatening to overflow.

He spoke to her in a hushed tone and motioned for her to have a seat in the living room then he led me into the kitchen.

The chicken continued to simmer appealingly in wine sauce, but the food has lost its appeal. Our once romantic dinner for two had just turned into an awkward party of three. Or maybe it was still a date for two--the two of them.

He pulled me into his arms and hugged me. A muffled sob escaped my throat. 'Aiden. Your name's Aiden,' I told him.

He nodded, recognition crossing his face. 'Yes, Aiden.'

Tears leaked from my eyes and streamed down my cheeks.

He patted my back and then released me. 'I'm sorry, Ashlyn, but I need to talk to her. Do you mind if...' He tipped his head toward the living room.

My heart constricted painfully in my chest. 'Of course. Go to her.'

I grabbed my bag and fled the apartment, unable to bear witness to their touching reunion. He had her name tattooed on his fucking arm. You didn't do that for just anyone.

I headed straight for the corner bar at the end of the street. I needed alcohol, and I needed it now.

Chapter Nineteen

I stumbled home much later feeling worse than I had when I left home, if that was even possible. I tried unsuccessfully to jam my key into the lock at least seven times when the door pulled open. A sleepy-eyed, shirtless Logan--I mean Aiden--stood in the doorway. He pulled me inside and against his chest and hugged me. His warm scent enveloped me in a comforting embrace.

'You're still here,' I commented, unable to keep the surprise from my voice.

'And you're drunk,' he whispered, his voice deep from sleep. I realized then that he was holding me upright, keeping me from tumbling headfirst over the pile of shoes near my door.

He guided me into the living room, and sat me down on the couch. 'I'll get you some water.' He turned and headed to the kitchen. 'And some aspirin,' he called over his shoulder.

I kicked off my shoes and laid my head against the back of the sofa. What was he still doing here? I assumed he'd be gone. I stared up at the ceiling, which seemed to be spinning in a circular pattern at the moment. I squeezed my eyes shut.

'Open,' Aiden said. I opened my eyes and saw him holding two white pills in front of me. I opened my mouth and he placed the aspirin on my tongue and tipped the water glass to my lips. I tilted my head back, swallowing the water and pills in one big gulp.

'I thought you'd be gone,' I said, wiping my mouth with the back of my hand.

He let out a deep sigh. 'I wouldn't have just left without talking to you first.'

Oh. 'So you still intend to leave, just not until after you've talked to me.'

He sighed and rubbed his hands across his face. 'Fuck, this is complicated, Ashlyn.'

'What's so complicated? You either want to be here with me, or you want to go with her. Simple.'

'That's what's crazy. I don't have any emotional connection to Logan.'

'You have her fucking name tattooed on your arm!' I shouted.

He pulled me by my upper arms until I was pressed up against him on the sofa. 'I don't even know her,' he growled.

My heart pounded in my chest. I swallowed and looked longingly at his mouth.

He released my arms, separating us, and our connection. 'But she holds the key to my past.'

I suddenly felt more sober. 'So...you need to go to her and figure all this out.'

'Ashlyn,' he growled, frustrated by my tone. 'You've been....you *are* everything to me. But you deserve more. If I could figure out who I am, stop having nightmares every night, get my life together...I have to try.'

I nodded. I couldn't deny him that chance, even if it would rip my heart from my chest to see him go.

'When are you leaving?' I asked.

He didn't answer right away, but even in the darkened room, I could see him frowning.

'Stay tonight. Don't leave me tonight,' I whispered, shuffling to get closer and climbing onto his lap. I guess I was the needy puppy now.

'Ashlyn,' his tone was frustrated, but he didn't push me away.

'Please,' I begged. It seemed to work on him before.

He rearranged my body so that I was straddling him. 'We shouldn't,' he breathed against my lips. 'There's too much to figure out right now...'

I didn't care that he was right. In that moment, I didn't even care that he'd probably be leaving in the morning. I needed him. I was blinded by my lust for him.

I kissed him harder than ever before, thrusting my tongue inside his mouth, biting his bottom lip to pull him towards me and nibbling his tongue when it met mine. It was partly the vodka I'd consumed, and partly my unadulterated hunger for him.

He didn't hold back. His hands roamed under my shirt and his fingertips danced across my ribs, and over my bra.

I ran my fingers through his hair and over the stubble on his jaw. I wanted to memorize every detail. The roughness of his jaw, the scent of his light, yet spicy aftershave, the way he made my stomach dance with butterflies when he kissed me.

I worked my hands under his shirt, loving the feel of his solid stomach, rippled with taut muscles. I had the strange urge to acknowledge our twin tattoos. I ran my fingers across his ribs, gripping the skin there as if to remind him. He let out a grunt.

My numb fingers quickly cooperated to unbutton his jeans. I worked my hand inside his boxers, feeling his hardened shaft and released a groan myself.

I tugged his jeans lower on his hips, exposing him to my caresses. He rocked against my hands, taking all the pleasure he could.

He lifted my top over my head and pulled it off, tossing it to the floor. I sat on his lap, in just my bra and jeans and looked at him in the moonlight. This was possibly my last time to see him like this, but I couldn't think about that right now or I would cry.

A sense of urgency struck me, and I began unbuttoning my jeans. I rose from his lap and thrust them down over my hips. His eyes followed my movements, watching my striptease. I pulled my undies down next, and deposited them on the floor with my jeans. I perched over him and he tugged me to him with his hands firmly on my ass.

I landed squarely on his lap with his cock pressing against me. I ground against him, moaning. I wanted to feel him fill me up and own me, even if it was only for tonight.

I moved from his lap again, this time perching on my knees to take him into my mouth. His cock caused my jaw to stretch to capacity, and I opened wider, willing him deeper. Tonight he was mine.

I licked and sucked his swollen head with enthusiasm, planting soft kisses against him.

He grunted and pushed his hips forward to meet my eager mouth. Each time he entered my mouth, I moaned around his thick shaft, and felt myself growing wet.

After several minutes, he pulled me up from my knees and back up to his lips. He began kissing me and bumping against my entrance with his cock. 'I want to fuck you, Ashlyn,' he murmured.

I groaned and helped him position himself so he began to slide into me. 'Oh, Logan,' I moaned.

He stiffened. 'Aiden,' he reminded me.

Oh, shit. I'd just called out her name. It instantly killed my libido, and I lifted myself off him.

'This is too strange, isn't it?' he asked.

I didn't answer. Instead, I found my panties on the floor and pulled them up my legs as if to prove my point. Yes, this was fucking weird.

He lifted his hips to slide his boxers and pants back into place and then stood. 'I'm sorry. I didn't mean for this to happen.'

'I know,' I mumbled, while tears filled my eyes. 'Just go. Go do what you need to do.'

He kissed my forehead, and then was gone. Just as quickly as he'd come into my life, he left. I curled against the couch and sobbed.

Chapter Twenty

The next month passed by in an agonizing charade of classes, research papers, and Liz's tough-love seminars only to fall into my empty bed each night to cry myself to sleep. I'd refused to change the sheets that still smelled like him.

I should have been ecstatic about my paper on amnesia being featured in next month's *Psychology Matters*, but I was too torn up over losing Aiden. I found myself wishing, not for the first time, that I was the one with amnesia. Forgetting all the painful memories and dumping them into oblivion would be damn nice. Sadly life was a cruel bastard, and so, of course, I didn't miraculously forget the pain.

I didn't forget the feeling of him climbing into bed late at night after painting and curling his body around mine, or the sleepy way he'd wake me up with kisses against the back of my neck in the morning. I didn't even forget the scent of his shaving cream in the steamy bathroom after his shower, since like a masochist who loves pain, I began buying the same brand he had and using it to shave my legs.

In other small ways, I'd learned how to live with the aching hole in my heart. The first step had been getting rid of all those damn paintings of Logan. Those found a nice home in the dumpster behind my building. I considered having an exorcism and burning them, but I couldn't bring myself to so blatantly destroy something he had created. I had also finally asked Liz to take in Tom since seeing him pawing at the door was a daily reminder of how domestic my life had become with Aiden. Liz had agreed and her cats now completely outnumbered her at three to one.

The sudden disappearance of Aiden from my life had caused feelings from long ago to resurface. My mom had been ripped from my life when I was six years old due to a car accident, and I found myself calling my dad more often than before, just to say hello or check on him. He might never be the man I wanted him to be, but he was still my dad, and I loved him.

My phone buzzed against the dining room table. Liz had insisted that tonight was my reintroduction into the wild, and I knew I couldn't ignore her any longer. I lifted various stacks of paper in an attempt to locate the device. I checked the caller ID, but it wasn't a number I recognized. I set the phone back down and continued working, hoping to finish my email to the master's student upset about her grade on Clancy's midterm before Liz called saying she was here to pick me up.

After clicking send on the email, I went to change. It was now securely fall in Chicago and last weekend I'd unpacked all my sweaters and scarves from the linen box under my bed. I pulled on a pair of dark-washed jeans, and a fitted gray knit sweater. I knew Liz would complain, but whatever. If I was being forced to go out tonight, I was going to be comfortable. I pulled on my brown boots on over the skinny jeans.

Expecting to hear my phone again, I couldn't place the noise at first. It was the doorbell. Someone was buzzing me from downstairs. Liz had arrived already. I jogged to the door and punched the call button. 'Be down in a sec, Liz.'

'Ashlyn?' his voice broke through the silence, and straight into my heart.

Aiden.

I pulled open the door, and rushed down the stairs toward the sound of his voice. The anticipation of seeing him for the first time in a month had me tingling all over. However, my excitement quickly faded away, to be replaced by fear. What if he was here to tell me he was officially back with Logan? I hesitated for a second before opening the door and drew a deep breath. I was strong. I could do this. And even if turned out I couldn't, there was always alcohol to numb the pain.

When I stepped outside Aiden was leaning against the side of the building looking down at the pavement deep in thought. He lifted his head and spotted me, a slow smile spreading across his lips. I wanted to rush to him, to throw my arms around his neck, to breathe in the scent of his chest, but my feet stayed planted to the sidewalk. He curled his hands into fists, and slowly released them, causing the veins in his forearms to stand out. Looking into his eyes, I noticed that the skin beneath them was marked by dark circles. Had he been sleeping? I pushed the thought from my mind. That wasn't my concern anymore. He had chosen to leave.

He didn't say anything for the first several seconds, he just stood perfectly still watching me like I was the most fascinating thing in the world. Well-dressed and clean shaven, wearing dark jeans, a fitted button-down shirt and dark jacket, he looked good. Aside from that though, I could tell things hadn't been going smoothly for him. His eyes were stormy and shadowed with darkened hollows.

'Hi,' I finally offered, feeling self-conscious under his scrutiny.

The expression on his face softened, and he let out a nervous chuckle low under his breath. 'Hi.'

I let myself take a deep breath and felt some of the tension evaporate from my shoulders.

His eyes wandered from mine, down to my chest, over hips and legs, and settling on my calves clad in the boots he was once so fond of. He swallowed roughly. 'You look well.'

'Thank you,' I replied in a clipped tone. *Why was he here?*

He looked at my outfit and frowned. 'Were you headed somewhere?'

I shook my head. 'I was going to meet Liz, but…just wait right here.' I sprinted up the stairs and grabbed my phone. I typed out a terribly misspelled text telling Liz that something had come up and I would explain later then raced back down the stairs.

He was standing on the sidewalk several feet from where I left him. 'Will you join me on a walk? I was hoping we could talk.'

We need to talk could be code for *thanks for making sure I wasn't homeless, it was nice knowing you*, or it could be code for *be mine forever and have my babies*. My stomach twisted into a painful knot. 'Sure,' I managed.

The sun was beginning its nightly descent and the sky was burnished a lovely shade of pink. I had no idea where we were headed, but I resisted breaking his concentration and instead followed beside him, trying to match his determined pace.

We reached what looked like a school and Logan stopped and stood in front of the building.

'What are we doing here?' I looked at him.

He took me by the shoulders, turning me to the right. My breath caught in my throat. It was his mural. I'd recognize his style anywhere. I began walking toward it, needing to get closer.

From left to right, I followed along the wall, trailing my hand as I walked. There was a path through a forest with warped, gnarled trees. It was dark and forbidding. As I walked, the painting got lighter and at the end of the path was a group of several people, of every age and race. They were lending helping hands, supporting each other, some were embracing. Its message of love and hope was clear. In script lettering at the bottom of the mural, it read: *You choose.*

I stood back in awed silence, admiring his work. He came up behind me and placed his hands on my shoulders. 'It's beautiful,' I commented.

He steered my shoulders to the edge of the wall. 'This is what I wanted to show you.'

He bent down near the wall and pointed to some lettering that could only be seen up close. I crouched down to inspect it.

He had translated our shared Latin tattoo and painted it in delicate black ink. *I will either find a way or make one.* Underneath that, his finger traced the words. *For Ashlyn, with love. Always.*

It was a very sweet gesture, and I was truly touched, but still I need to hear him, in his own words, tell me what he was doing back here, why he had been away for a month. I wouldn't allow myself to get my hopes up. I stood up and dusted the soil off my knees.

After looking at the mural we walked along Lakeshore Drive. The gusts from Lake Michigan made the air feel colder, but the crisp breeze washed over me and left me revived.

Aiden saw me hugging my arms around my chest, and started to remove his jacket.

'No, you keep it.' When I stopped him, my fingers brushed against his. It was an innocent touch, but still caused a swell of longing to surge through me. My skin tingled in awareness of him. My damn body was betraying me.

'You're cold. Let's stop and get a drink.' He tipped his head to the jazz club directly across the street from where we stood. I nodded and we made our way to it.

Once we were seated directly across from each other at the tiny pedestal table with a flickering red candle between us, I nibbled on my bottom lip. Surely this was it; we were going to have The Conversation now. Just then the server appeared and Aiden placed our drink order. A bottle of Bordeaux that he said was apparently his favorite and he wanted me to try it.

When our wine came, he signaled the server to pour me the first taste. I brought the glass to my lips while Aiden watched and took a small sip. I swirled the rich, fragrant liquid across my tongue and swallowed. It was tangy and tart with notes of berry. He was right, I loved it. I nodded and the server filled my glass, and then his.

I took another sip of my wine, noting my skin had already warmed from the combination of Logan's proximity, and the delicious wine.

'What have you been doing for the past month?' I inwardly cringed, afraid he would answer with a single word that would crush me: Logan.

His hazel eyes locked on mine, looking insanely intense. 'Putting together the pieces of my life. Trying to become whole again.'

Another healthy gulp of wine had me feeling more like my old self, comfortable and at ease in his presence. 'And, what did you find? Do you have a house in the suburbs? An apartment in the city? Wife? Dog? Two-point-five kids?'

He frowned and set down his wine glass. 'I live alone in a loft just north of the city. It's cold and sterile. You'd hate it. Hell, I hate it. I've grown used to your messy, lived-in apartment.'

'Did you just call me messy?' I teased. I surprised myself with my ability to appear so calm about this, while inside my stomach was in knots.

'Not you.' He reached across the table and squeezed my hand. 'Your apartment.'

The sudden contact and warmth of his skin made me shudder and I pulled my hand back. 'How could no one have been looking for you? I don't understand.'

A pained expression crossed his face for a brief second before his eyes found mine and cleared again. 'I grew up in foster care, so I don't really have a family. I'm still connected with a few of

137

my foster siblings, but we don't talk often. And I was on sabbatical from the university, so my colleagues didn't think anything of it.'

He truly was alone. I wondered if that made it harder or easier for him to slip back into his old life.

The conversation was flowing so well between us, that I almost didn't want to bring her up. Almost. 'And Logan?'

He let out a deep sigh. 'Where to begin…' He strummed against the tabletop with his long fingers.

'At the beginning?' I suggested, helpfully.

He smiled at me. 'Are you sure you want to hear about this?'

I nodded. I didn't so much *want* to as I needed to.

'I met her in Memphis that summer I worked down there, and it turned out she was from Chicago too, which sort of bonded us together in a place far from home. She was taking a metalworks seminar, and neither of us knew a soul there.

'It turned out she fled to Memphis trying to get away from an ex-boyfriend with a drug problem. She was clean, had been for a while, but she admitted she had a weakness for alpha males and cocaine. At first I wanted nothing to do with her, but as we spent time together I began to trust that all of that was really behind her.

'We dated for three years. I guess I thought I could save her, change her.' He shook his head. 'And I did. For a while. But then she started slipping. About two years in to our relationship, she hit a mental block with her art, and everything started to fall apart.

'She started using again, and began hanging out with her old crowd. That day in the warehouse, we'd broken up and she'd called me frantically, asking me to help her. She owed money to a dealer. That's how I ended up at that warehouse that day, trying to bail her out of trouble. I don't remember exactly what happened when I got there. But …I guess you know how it ended.'

I nodded. 'Did she come looking for you?'

'I'd told her during that last phone call that I was done, and for her not to call me again. She went back to rehab and had no idea what had happened to me.'

I swallowed another gulp of wine, hoping to dislodge the lump from my throat before asking my next question. 'So if you guys were…broken up…does that mean…?'

His brows pulled together. 'I'm not with Logan. That's what you thought this was about? Me leaving?'

I nodded, tears filling my eyes at the mention of the way he'd left me.

'Christ, Ashlyn, no.'

He squeezed my hand again and waited for me to regain my composure, not wanting to upset me any further. I appreciated that. I didn't cry in public.

'I've talked to her pretty much every day for the last month, but only because she seems to know me, I mean the old me, better than anyone. I don't feel anything for her.'

My body visibly sagged with relief. The effects of the wine and seeing Aiden again after so long had left my emotions frayed and raw. I knew if he left again it would take a hell of a lot more than crying on Liz's shoulder and a few shots of vodka to fix me. Everything was clicking into place. Memphis. The street sign we couldn't place in Chicago. Even the blues music.

I gripped my hands in my lap and stared up at him. 'Why did you come back?' We might as well end this little charade of the happy reunion now. I couldn't betray my feelings for him until I knew exactly why he was here. I couldn't be rejected again.

He rubbed the back of his neck the way I'd seen him do when he got nervous. What did he have to be nervous about?

'I know I don't deserve a woman like you. My upbringing was less than stellar, and my past relationships were…questionable, but keeping myself away from you for the last month was the hardest damn thing I've ever done. And I know there's still so much you don't know about me…'

I knew him better than anyone. I knew he was kind, and sweet, and hard working. And that he liked steamed milk in his coffee, and that if I was ever in a trivia game involving history questions, I'd make damn sure he was on my team. I knew that he made me incredibly hot, and nothing would change my mind about wanting to be with him.

'When two people begin dating, do they know every little detail about one another?' I challenged.

'No,' he answered sheepishly.

'Then what is it that you think I need to know?'

He thought about it for a second, then smirked. 'My middle name is James,' he said simply. 'And I'm twenty-seven.'

I smiled. 'Aiden James York.' It had a nice ring to it. 'It's nice to meet you.'

He brought my outstretched hand to his lips and laid a damp kiss on my palm.

Chapter Twenty-One

If I didn't get the key in the lock on this next try, I thought Aiden would break the damn door down. Although if he hadn't been pressed up against my backside grinding his erection against me, I might not have been so distracted.

'Move,' he growled, taking the key from my hand. He thrust it into the lock and turned. I nearly moaned in relief. My entire body needed him. We'd made out in the backseat of the cab the entire ride back, happy and drunk from our shared conversation and bottle of wine.

Once inside, he flipped on the lights and took my face in his big warm hands, and just looked at me lovingly. 'Being here with you, in this tiny apartment, you were everything I needed. I thought I needed more--to know everything about my past. I was wrong. You were all I thought about, all I needed. Nothing compared to you. Not the money in my bank account, my job at the university, my lavish apartment. I'd trade it all to have you back.'

'Yes. Please.'

We began a disjointed dance of tugging at each other's clothing, desperate to be closer. Aiden seemed reluctant to remove my boots, but my jeans were tucked inside them, so it was necessary. Then he knelt before me and peeled off my socks, kissing the soles of both feet before standing to remove my shirt. In my jeans, bra and bare feet, I felt more beautiful than ever. His intense gaze never left me. He slid his fingertip under the waistband of my jeans and circled my hipbone, his finger dancing lightly over my tattoo, sending a delicate flush all the way up to my chest.

I pulled his jacket off his shoulders, letting it fall to the floor and he pulled his shirt off over his head. His bare chest was one of my favorite things about him. I could stare at his muscled pecs and stomach all day. After a few moments, though, I realized he was just standing there, not moving. I glanced up at him and he was grinning at me expectantly, like he was waiting for something. I tilted my head to the side slightly and surveyed him.

Then I saw it, and my heart squeezed in my chest.

The tattoo on his bicep that had once read *Logan* had been covered up with an intricate tribal design that hid the text underneath it entirely. I ran my fingertips across it and stared at him in awe.

'Do you like it, sweetheart?'

I nodded.

We would both still know it was there, but maybe that was okay. Logan was part of our shared history. I didn't want to admit it, but sometimes it was still hard for me to think of him as Aiden. Aiden James, I reminded myself.

Once we were undressed, he arranged the throw pillows and blanket from the sofa on the floor, and gently lowered me on top of the makeshift bed. He placed his hand on my belly and gently pushed me back until I was lying down. Despite our one-month separation, he took his time, gently suckling and kissing my breasts before heading south.

I was wet and needy by the time his lips reached my sex. I moaned in sweet relief when he finally kissed me there. I opened my eyes and watched as he made love to me with his mouth. His tongue swirled in a familiar, delicious pattern, delivering as much pleasure as he could. He gently nibbled and sucked, seemingly enamored with this activity. I loved watching him, and soon I was moaning and arching against his mouth with each exquisite flick of his tongue.

'Aiden,' I groaned as my release came.

He kissed my bare mound several more times before removing himself from in between my legs. I loved how I no longer felt self-conscious about being completely exposed to him.

I shifted to my knees to take him into my mouth, but his hand on my elbow stopped me. He shook his head. 'Come here, beautiful. I need to be inside you.'

I smiled at his words.

He pulled me to his lap so I was straddling him. He held my hips just above his cock and encouraged me to sink down onto him. 'I want you to fuck me, baby.'

I lowered myself down and immediately felt the resistance of his thick erection trying to penetrate me. He reached between us and grabbed his cock, dipping and swirling it in my wetness to try and ease its entrance.

'You okay, sweetheart?'

I nodded.

He pushed inside me slowly, inch by delicious inch until I was stretched to capacity and my head dropped back, arching against the mix of pleasure and slight sting of pain.

Once he had buried himself in me fully, he let out a deep moan from the back of his throat and I opened my eyes to watch him. His pupils were dilated with pleasure and desire. He was beautiful. And he was mine.

His pace slowed to an easy rhythm, and he grinned as he met my eyes. 'I love you, Ashlyn.'

'I love you too.'

He pulled me close, nuzzling into my neck and planting kisses up and down my throat.

I lifted myself off him and began sliding up and down.

'Ah…' he breathed. 'Fuck, baby, that's good.'

His sexy murmurings spurred me on and I moved faster against him.

His hands roamed my skin, fingertips running along my arms, tickling down my sides, and then trailing lightly up my naked spine. He cupped the back of my neck and brought my mouth to his in a crushing kiss. I loved his forwardness and the way he took command of my body. It was his for the taking.

His gripped my waist, his fingers biting into the skin as he pulled me in closer. I cried out and let him move me into whichever position suited him best. He clutched my ass in his palms and nibbled on my bare shoulder.

I was completely uninhibited and let my body have its way. With each downward thrust, I felt him bump against me and I knew I wouldn't be able to hold off my second orgasm long. He gripped my hips and guided me up and down, loud, breathy moans escaping his parted lips.

'Aiden, I'm going to come.'

'Me too, baby.' With his hand on the back of my neck, he guided my mouth to his and kissed me quickly.

I tossed my head back and whimpered. I continued thrusting against him, and felt as he released into me. My relief quickly followed, with an intense throbbing pleasure deep inside me.

After I had finished bouncing against him, he held me firmly against his chest and brushed my hair back from my face. I was about to apologize or at least try to say something cute about my uninhibited performance when he bit his lip and tilted his head toward the door.

'Um, baby…' he said, his expression one of concern.

I heard the sound of a throat clearing from across the room.

Liz was leaning against the far wall, a box of crackers in her hand, happily munching away and watching us put on a show.

'Liz! What the hell?'

Aiden only chuckled. He pulled out from inside me and covered me with his discarded T-shirt that lay next to us on the floor. Only that meant he was left completely exposed, but he didn't seem to mind.

Liz's lips curled up in a devilish grin. 'Damn. You let him put that whole thing inside you?' she asked, eyeing his still-hard cock.

'Liz!' I screamed. It was so not okay that she was practically drooling over his erection. A surge of jealousy swelled up inside me. 'Cover that damn thing up,' I shouted at Aiden. I mean, I got that he was proud of it, and rightly so, but that didn't mean anyone but me was allowed to see it. And damn if it wasn't standing there in all its glory, proudly announcing that Aiden and I were back together.

'How long have you been here?' I demanded, tugging his T-shirt over my head. My hair was currently sporting a just fucked look, but that was the least of my worries.

'A few minutes, tops. And shit, you guys were *hot*.'

'A few minutes!' I released a frustrated huff.

'I didn't want to interrupt your orgasm,' she explained, pouring herself a glass of wine from the bottle on my counter. 'It's what any good friend would do in this situation.'

Aiden chuckled again and grabbed his jeans and boxer briefs, holding them in front of his manhood, and shuffled off for the bathroom. He reemerged with his pants riding low on his hips and his chest bare, still looking entirely too sexy for Liz's viewing pleasure. Of course he was still smiling, like none of this even remotely bothered him.

'What are you doing here?' I'd forgotten about the spare key I'd given to her when Aiden had moved out. I snatched the box of crackers from her and set them roughly on the counter.

'You sort of bailed out on me without an explanation tonight. Then you weren't answering your phone. I came to check on you. Make sure you hadn't slit your wrists or done anything stupid.'

Aiden winced and immediately pulled me closer to him.

'Sorry, um, I was…'

'Having hot, sweaty sex. Yeah, I saw that and you're forgiven.' She finished the wine in a single gulp. 'But you.' She pointed at Aiden. 'If you ever hurt her like that again, I'll personally hunt you down and cut your balls off with a rusty butter knife.'

He gulped and held me protectively in front of him.

'You planning on sticking around this time?' Liz asked, fixing him with her gaze.

'I'll marry her tomorrow if she'll let me,' he answered, his voice not wavering in the slightest.

I turned to face him and saw that without a doubt, he was serious. He cupped my face and held my eyes with his. 'Will you, baby? Marry me?' I tried to answer, to say something, but emotion had robbed me of my voice. Tears spilled over and rolled down my cheeks.

He brushed the tears away with his fingertips. 'Not today, not tomorrow, but someday soon?'

I merely nodded and his lips were back on mine. His kiss was anything but innocent, and I quickly forgot about our company when his tongue began flirting with mine.

Liz laughed. 'As much as I'd love to stay and see a repeat of that earlier performance, I have a feeling I better go.'

We didn't even wait for the door to close. Aiden was already tugging the T-shirt over my head, and I lifted my arms to help him before the latch clicked. I reached down to unbutton his jeans, finding him hard and ready for me again.

He gazed into my eyes and stroked my bottom lip lovingly with his thumb. 'Mine,' he whispered.

'Yes, yours. Only yours. Always.'

Epilogue

One Month Later
Aiden

I looked around the empty loft one last time. It was strange to think I'd lived here for four years, yet felt zero connection to the place. The massive king bed was too firm, the kitchen gadgets too high-tech and the stiff leather furniture too modern to actually be comfortable.

After living in Ashlyn's cramped, yet homey apartment this place just seemed too cold, too clinical with its exposed duct work ceilings and concrete floors. I was glad to be moving on, moving away from the man I no longer knew, and towards the one I wanted to become.

I'd packed most of my clothes and personal belongings and decided the rest I could do without. I'd put the loft on the market fully furnished to my realtors surprise, just wanting to get rid of it all and start over.

My phone buzzed in my pocket and I reached down to fish it out while juggling the large duffle bag containing most of my belongings. *Shit*. It was Logan again.

I frowned and slide the phone back inside my pocket. It wasn't that I hadn't appreciated everything she'd told me about my former self – I had. I learned that I had a gym membership to a club downtown, and what topics I'd been most interested in teaching as a history professor, and even my favorite foods (sushi, and Mexican – in that order).

But the more time that passed without even a hint of my memory being restored, or me returning any feelings for her, the more persistent she became. And when I'd called her last night to tell her that Ashlyn and I were officially moving in together, she'd broken down in tears, so I left out the part where I'd sort of asked Ashlyn to marry me. It wasn't an official proposal yet anyways, so no sense in throwing salt in the wound.

Part of me felt bad for Logan – I mean obviously I had loved her deeply at one time, I had her name tattooed on my bicep for Christ's sake – but her past had come back to haunt us both and ultimately drove us apart. The other part of me realized that if I hadn't ended up with amnesia, I would have never met Ashlyn, a thought that did not sit well with me.

I closed and locked the door to my old loft – and my old life –one last time, eager to get back to my beautiful girl waiting for me at our new condo, and unable to keep a smile from crossing my lips at the mere thought.

Aut viam inveniam aut faciam tibi. I will either find a way, or make one.